"Thank yo

She hung on to the driver-side door. "You're welcome."

Chloe had been so kind to Lili, who was so attached to her teacher, to the cat, to Truelove.

Noah stuffed his hands in his pockets. "If it's okay with you, I'd like to finish the staircase at the Lyric."

Her eyes widened. "Do you mean it? Would you?"

Noah shuffled his feet. "If you still want me to."

"I still want you to."

Their gazes locked.

His heart skipped a beat. She blushed.

"Are you sure?"

"Lili can finish out the school year." He shrugged, aiming for a nonchalance he was far from feeling. "I'm sure."

"Thank you."

For a host of reasons, staying in Truelove was probably a bad idea. But as he and Lili got into his truck, he couldn't think of any place on earth he'd rather be.

Lisa Carter and her family make their home in North Carolina. In addition to her Love Inspired novels, she writes romantic suspense. When she isn't writing, Lisa enjoys traveling to romantic locales, teaching writing workshops and researching her next exotic adventure. She has strong opinions on barbecue and ACC basketball. She loves to hear from readers. Connect with Lisa at lisacarterauthor.com.

Visit the Author Profile page at LoveInspired.com for more titles.

BUILDING HER A HOME

LISA CARTER

LOVE INSPIRED
INSPIRATIONAL ROMANCE

LOVE INSPIRED®
INSPIRATIONAL ROMANCE

ISBN-13: 978-1-335-93733-9

Recycling programs
for this product may
not exist in your area.

Building Her a Home

Love Inspired
22 Adelaide St. West, 41st Floor
Toronto, Ontario M5H 4E3, Canada
www.LoveInspired.com

Printed in Lithuania

MIX
Paper | Supporting
responsible forestry
FSC® C021394

Now faith is the substance of things hoped for,
the evidence of things not seen.
—*Hebrews* 11:1

To my aunt Betsy.

Thank you for a beautiful example of a faith-filled life
and for always being there for me. I love you.

Chapter One

Chloe was a fixer. A rescuer. Her greatest joy was helping other people and bringing them happiness.

Which was why, on a glorious blue-sky, early April afternoon, she was climbing one of the oak trees lining the square in her hometown of Truelove, North Carolina, trying to rescue a cat for a little girl.

High above the ground, she reached for the cat, but with a flick of its tail, the feline bounded onto another branch, evading her grasp once again.

Chloe's family accused her of rushing into situations without thinking things through first. Leaping before she looked.

Wobbling, she only just managed to catch hold of the trunk and regain her balance. Her heart pounded.

At twenty-seven, climbing a tree wasn't as effortless as she remembered. Nor had she factored in how far away the ground appeared from her precarious position in the treetop.

Lili's anxious blue eyes peered through the canopy of leafed-out branches. "Please, Miss Randolph." Tendrils of her dark hair, braided in pigtails, fluttered in the slight breeze. "Help Felix before he gets hurt."

Felix wasn't the only one in danger of getting hurt. But she would do anything for one of her students. The tuxedo cat had a black body with a white chest that resembled men's formalwear. She frowned at the feline, but Felix settled onto the branch and started grooming himself.

"Don't worry, Lili," she called to the four-year-old. "I'm almost there."

Octogenarian IdaLee Redfern gazed up at Chloe. "This isn't safe, dear heart."

Her snow-white hair gleaming in the sunshine, the retired former schoolteacher exchanged a worried glance with her best friend, ErmaJean Hicks.

Never-met-a-stranger ErmaJean beckoned. "Maybe let the fire department handle this, sugar."

Perhaps this hadn't been Chloe's best idea. But when she discovered Lili standing forlorn under the tree with the silver-haired older women of the Double Name Club, Chloe started climbing without giving it a second thought.

Also known as the Truelove Matchmakers, the ladies were her mentors. Master practitioners in the art of helping people find happiness. Less charitable citizens believed they took the town motto—*Truelove, Where True Love Awaits*—a little too seriously. But sensing in Chloe a kindred spirit, the often misunderstood ladies had taken her under their wing.

In addition to her work as a music therapist—and mounting cat rescue operations—Chloe was a matchmaker in training. Last week, she set up a blind date for the town veterinarian with a local dairy farmer.

Clinging to the oak, she made a mental note to check with Ingrid about how the evening had gone. Of course, not everyone understood the sacred calling of the matchmakers. Her brother Jeffrey liked to say she was overly involved in other people's lives and not enough in her own. *Ouch.* Although… not entirely inaccurate.

She glanced down. Clusters of daffodils nodded in the spring breeze. A crowd had gathered across the graveled paths of the square.

Patrons of nearby Mason Jar Café had turned out to watch the ensuing drama unfold. Until she could complete her other big project—the restoration of the historic movie theater into an arts center—this was what constituted high entertainment in the small Blue Ridge town of Truelove.

Several townspeople recorded her latest shenanigans on their cell phones. Her most recent escapade would not only be all over Truelove, but splashed across social media as well. Her older brothers would not be pleased with her. Not pleased at all.

From her perch, she had a bird's-eye view of the perpetually smoky-blue mist from which the mountains surrounding the Appalachian community derived its name. Gushing with run-off from melted snow, the river bended around the town like a horseshoe.

Behind her lay the shops on Main Street. To the west, the fire department and school. The town hall was located on the south end of the square. And on the north end, the iconic Lyric Theater she was working so hard to bring back to life.

A tall, lanky man broad-shouldered his way through the throng. Not getting a good look at his face, she could only see the top of his dark, short-cropped hair. Stopping beside the matchmakers, he bent his head to speak to the diminutive IdaLee.

Or was he talking to Lili?

Angular and with a short cap of iron-gray hair, GeorgeAnne Allen, the no-nonsense leader of the Double Name Club, clamped her hands on the bony hips of her jeans. "Come down at once, Chloe."

Taking a deep breath, she adjusted her grip. "I've got this, Miss GeorgeAnne."

Married, divorced or spinster, "Miss" was an honorary title of respect bestowed on every elder Southern lady.

Balancing her weight on the balls of her feet, she stretched out her hands. "Almost there…" Pouncing, she scooped the cat into her arms. Felix yowled in protest. Grinning with triumph, she cuddled the feline against her blouse. The cat writhed.

Her foot slipped. Below, there was a collective gasp of breath. Falling, she clawed at the air. This had been a bad idea. A very bad idea indeed.

Leaves slapping her face, she crashed through the branches. The ground rushed up to meet her. Chloe screamed.

Stepping forward, the man caught her in his arms. Her momentum knocked them into the trunk of the tree. Taking the brunt of the impact, he grunted. Snarling, the cat leaped away, landing nimbly on its feet.

"Are you okay, ma'am?"

Nodding, the woman brushed the wavy mass of dark brown hair out of her eyes. Noah got a glimpse of warm, chocolate brown eyes before she stiffened and whispered something.

In that split second, he became aware of two things, one following on the heels of the other so swiftly as to be almost simultaneous.

She smelled like honeysuckle. And he knew her from somewhere.

Then, they were set upon by the concerned onlookers. She was plucked out of his arms by the tallest of the trio of older women on the committee, who'd hired him three months ago to restore the historic gazebo on the square.

Engulfed by the townspeople, he lost sight of her. But he found Lili at the edge of the crowd, crouching near a park bench. She stroked the cat with the tip of her forefinger.

"Careful." He squatted beside his niece. "The stray had a scare. He doesn't know you. You might get hurt."

She tilted her head, gazing at him from those solemn blue eyes of hers, so like the sister he'd lost far too early. "Felix wouldn't hurt me. We're friends."

Noah had spent the last four years making sure nothing

and no one ever hurt her. It had been just the two of them for as long as Lili could remember. But friends—as in the lack thereof—had become a recurring theme with her.

He'd hoped, by enrolling her in the preschool program in Truelove, to satisfy her yearning for companionship. A temporary measure until they left for his next job. She was getting old enough to wonder why they moved from town to town. Why other kids had a mom and a dad. Why she had only a Noah.

She was his entire world. Yet he sensed he was no longer enough for her rapidly expanding curiosity. He knew first-hand how cruel a place the world could be. He'd dedicated his life to protecting her from it. Yet he was beginning to realize not even the best parent could totally insulate a child from life's harshest realities.

Like the death of her mother.

"Come on, Lil. It's quitting time for me. Dinnertime for you."

"I can't leave Felix." She shook her head. The braids he'd carefully plaited this morning swung from side to side. "Felix needs me. Felix is lonely. Felix is hungry."

What Lili meant was, *she* needed Felix. *She* was lonely.

He scrubbed his face with his hand. "We'll drive to the hamburger place on the highway. You love the french fries there."

Crossing her arms over her small body, she set her pointed little chin at him. "Felix likes french fries, too."

He blew out a breath. "You can't have a pet. The motel doesn't allow animals."

She pursed her mouth. "Why can't we live in a house? Felix loves houses."

"Because we go where my job takes us. Not every little girl gets to see the Pacific Ocean or ride a swan boat in Boston. Isn't that great?"

"Other girls have pets." A pucker creased the smoothness of her forehead. "They have a family."

"I'm your family."

She frowned. "It's not the same."

He was failing her, and it gutted him.

A shadow fell across them.

He glanced up to find ErmaJean Hicks standing over them. A volunteer at the preschool, her kindness had been a godsend. Every afternoon, the older woman walked Lili from the extended day program across the street to Noah at the gazebo, as he ended work for the day. It had been Lili's cries for help that had drawn him to the tree.

ErmaJean's denim-blue eyes twinkled. "I'm glad you found each other."

Hissing, the cat arched its back and streaked away. Lili reached for the beast, but it was gone in a flash.

"It's for the best, Lili." He crossed his arms over his shirt. "I'm finishing the gazebo in a few days, and we'll be moving on."

Her chin wobbled. "But I like it here."

She started to cry. A self-contained, stoic little person, Lili rarely cried.

He pulled her against him. Squeezing her eyes shut, she turned her face into his jean-clad thigh.

Noah liked it here, too. It would be easy to get attached to the town. With its undulating blue-green ridges fanning across the horizon, Truelove was a pretty place with friendly people.

But he was born to wander. A nomad at heart. "I don't know what's got into her."

ErmaJean placed her hand on Lili's head. "School and aftercare make for a long day. Tired and hungry is a bad combination."

Guilt pressed hard on his chest, making it difficult to draw an even breath. "I'm a terrible parent."

"You're too hard on yourself. Lili is always neat as a pin.

It's obvious she is well cared for and much loved. You give her what every child needs most."

"Except a home." Swallowing, he glanced away. The crowd had dissipated.

"I think you'll discover home is wherever the ones we love the most are found." She patted his arm. "Perhaps after supper, you two could find Felix and give him a hamburger patty of his own."

"Could we?" Lili whispered. The hope in her eyes—the trust that he could fix anything—was a gift he didn't take for granted.

"Sure, Lili-bell."

The smile she bestowed upon him was radiant.

He took Lili's hand. "Thank you, Miss ErmaJean."

The older woman gave Lili a hug. "I'll see you tomorrow at school."

Lili waved goodbye.

Exhausted from a long day at work, nevertheless, he went through the drive-through and drove back to Truelove. He insisted Lili eat her dinner before they got out of his truck. Which she did, under protest.

Twilight was fast approaching by the time they located the pesky creature, hanging around the shuttered bakery. The sidewalks rolled up in Truelove at the close of the business day. They had Main Street to themselves.

Before the cat could skitter away, Lili showed him the beef. Felix meowed.

With imperious dignity, the cat waited for Lili to tear the hamburger into smaller pieces. She knelt beside him.

Noah leaned against the bakery wall while the cat ate its fill. Who knew why she'd christened him Felix? Yet it was obvious from her shining eyes she was happy. Which made him happy.

Abruptly deciding they'd enjoyed the pleasure of his company long enough, with a flick of his tail, the cat raced off into the night.

She clambered to her feet. "Felix!"

"The cat isn't pet material, Lil. He was born to be wild." Like him. The him he used to be.

He shoved off from the wall. "You'll probably see him tomorrow." Unfortunately. "It's time for bed."

She slipped her small hand into his calloused one. "Thank you," she whispered.

It was he who ought to be thanking her. When she was born, she'd changed his life forever. For the better.

At the motel, they read a story together. He sang her a song. She was the only one he sang for these days. She said her bedtime prayers.

It was their usual routine. It was everything to him. She was everything to him.

Later in the dark, when she slept in the twin bed adjacent to his, he stared at the cracked ceiling above his head. For the first time in a long time, loneliness like a reverberating chord echoed inside him.

It was only then he realized what the woman had whispered as he held her in his arms. Maybe he'd misheard. How could she possibly know his other name? The name from which he'd run.

Noah Knightley.

Yesterday, when she dropped into his arms, Chloe had recognized him right away.

He wouldn't remember her, of course. When their paths crossed at the summer music festival where she'd worked eight years ago, she'd had a huge crush on him. She'd been a nobody, a lowly college intern. He'd been handsome, incredibly gifted and already on his way to being famous.

In those days, he'd sported a beard and worn his hair long,

as befitted his bad-boy image. Yet despite his short hair-cut and clean-shaven appearance now, she'd know those oft-photographed, smoldering blue eyes of his anywhere. He had been a rising country music singer until mysteriously disappearing from the music scene.

Noah Knightley is the carpenter hired to rebuild True-love's gazebo?

She was amazed she'd never run into him before. A not-so-easy feat in a town the size of Truelove. But between her students, the arts center renovation and matchmaker training, she'd been too busy to take much notice of the itinerant carpenter working in the middle of the town green.

Chloe thrived on staying busy, though after yesterday's fiasco, she'd avoid any future cat rescues.

With the arts underfunded in most school districts, her services were shared between the elementary, the middle school and the high school. Her day often included driving all over the county.

But she loved watching her students find a connection to music. Like ten-year-old Christopher, whose muscular dystrophy confined him to a wheelchair. The bright-eyed boy had discovered a new confidence in playing the drums.

Or fourteen-year-old LaToya, in recovery from an eating disorder, finding new ways of coping with her sometimes chaotic emotions by performing her own musical compositions.

Chloe believed passionately in the transformative ability of music to change lives. To heal. To empower. And she loved being a part of the process.

Over the next few days, she did her best to avoid running into her erstwhile rescuer. It was embarrassing when one person remembered and the other one didn't. Yet now she was actively trying to avoid him, she somehow managed to run into him at the grocery store.

When he rounded the corner from the bread aisle, she made

a beeline for the produce section. She hunkered over the bin of root vegetables and prayed for him to leave without noticing her. It was a long ten minutes while he sorted through bananas. She loved her veggies as good as the next person, but honestly, cabbage wasn't that exciting.

Midafternoon on Thursday, she was finishing a group jam session in Mrs. Phillips's special needs classroom at the elementary school when her phone dinged with a text. Martha Alice Breckinridge, the chairperson of the Lyric Theater restoration, had called for an emergency committee meeting at the Jar ASAP.

Instead of taking the shortcut across the square—a route that would have brought her past the gazebo—she walked two full blocks around the square to reach the diner.

Standing on the sidewalk, she spotted him inside the café, sitting in a booth overlooking Main Street.

At his catch-the-breath handsomeness, a feeling not unlike butterflies fluttered in her rib cage. The same knee-buckling sensation she'd experienced at age nineteen. That summer, she'd made it a point to keep her distance. She'd left him to the other girls, jockeying to get to know him.

Stop being ridiculous.

Chloe was a grown woman with grown-up responsibilities, not an overgrown adolescent. The committee members were waiting on her.

Yet unable to resist, she took another look at him, and her heart did a traitorous quiver. The rugged jawline. The dreamy cheekbones. How did somebody get born that gorgeous?

He'd been kind to both megastars and nobodies like her. In an industry notable for its egos, he hadn't taken himself too seriously. He was the total package.

Totally out of her league.

Seeing him again, the niggling ember of dissatisfaction

with her current life—that she worked hard to keep at bay—threatened to burst into flame once more.

Chloe hitched her purse strap higher onto her shoulder. One more reason to steer clear of him. She entered the diner.

Above the door, a bell jingled. The enticing aroma of fresh baked bread wafted past her nostrils. Occupying a table near the back, Martha Alice lifted her hand to attract her attention.

Chloe picked her way among the cluster of linoleum-topped tables. Despite her resolve to ignore him, she couldn't prevent her gaze from wandering to his booth. His long, slim-fingered hands were wrapped around a white porcelain mug. The same long, slim-fingered hands she'd last seen on the fretboard of a guitar.

She slipped into the last unoccupied chair, giving her an all-too-clear line of sight to her former crush.

Martha Alice cleared her throat. "Now that everyone is here, I wanted to make you aware Delano Hampton will no longer be working on the Lyric."

Her heart sank. The other committee members appeared equally shocked.

GeorgeAnne Allen scowled. "What happened?"

Fellow matchmaker Martha Alice sighed. "Due to a family emergency, Delano has been forced to resign from the project."

Chloe's stomach knotted. This wasn't good news. Without his expertise, the entire project was in jeopardy.

Her friend, Kelsey McKendry a fundraising genius, turned to the Drake Construction manager. "What does this mean for our timetable?"

Colton Atkinson opened his hands. "It wrecks the timetable. Delano finished rebuilding the box seats in the main auditorium, but he hadn't tackled reconstructing the grand staircase, which is the final phase of the restoration."

Kelsey exchanged a look with her father, Boyd. "Will the music festival have to be postponed?"

"I don't see how the festival can go on." Boyd Summerfield shook his head. "The staircase *is* the Lyric. Without it, the main floor is incomplete." The Summerfield Group was a major capital investor in developing the Lyric Arts Center.

Chloe shuddered to think of the fundraising efforts gone to waste, the months of painstaking labor by the skilled team of artisans hired to return the Lyric to its Art Deco splendor.

Retired fire chief Rick MacKenzie frowned. "The festival is meant to fill the coffers of our scholarship fund. Is there no way Delano can be replaced?"

The scholarships would provide underserved, at-risk children and youth in the area access to the arts program.

"Chloe researched and hired the conservators," said Cliff Penry, CPA, pushing his glasses higher on the bridge of his nose. "How soon can we find a replacement with Delano's credentials?"

Everyone looked at her.

"Restoration artisans are often contractually obligated for months at a time on already ongoing projects." Her gaze landed on Noah Knightley. "Although, I may have an idea."

She dragged her eyes from the outline of his broad shoulders to the committee. "Give me twenty-four hours to find a solution."

Martha Alice clasped her hands to her chin. "I knew we could count on you."

She could fix this. It was what she did. It was who she was.

Chloe Randolph to the rescue.

With no further teaching assignments for the rest of the afternoon, she marched across Main Street to the square to inspect Noah's handiwork on the gazebo. Chin in hand, she circled the elaborate, octagonal structure. He'd done a masterful job of recreating the intricate scrollwork on the Victorian-inspired gingerbread trim.

Built at the turn of the twentieth century, the gazebo had been demolished in a spring tornado several years ago. After a long period of fundraising, the good ladies of the Double Name Club had launched a beautification committee and hired a preservation carpenter to restore the historic character of the town's most iconic feature.

He'd had to raze the temporary structure the town had utilized over the last several years. Starting from scratch, he'd rebuilt the gazebo from the foundation. Only a final coat of paint remained to complete the project.

She was more than a little curious how he'd gone from a string of chart-topping singles to carpentry in a small mountain town, but it was his woodworking skills she needed now. Desperately needed, if disaster were to be averted.

The young country music star had figured largely—more than she liked to admit—in the most thrilling summer of her life. But no matter how awkward, she had to find a way to fix the current crisis.

Her courage lasted just long enough for her return to the Mason Jar. But then she panicked. Nerves aflutter, heart thudding, she sank onto one of the cherry-red swivel stools lining the white, chrome-sided counter.

In the reflection of the security mirror mounted above the chalked menu board, she kept her eyes glued on the man in the booth behind her.

"See anything you like?"

Jolting, Chloe's eyes dropped from the mirror and onto Trudy McKendry's smiling countenance.

The Mason Jar manager withdrew a pencil tucked behind her ear. She tapped the pencil against her order pad. "What's your pleasure today, hon?"

"A slice of pecan pie, please," she whispered.

Trudy leaned over the counter. "Why are you whispering?"

"No reason." She cleared her throat. "Coffee, too."

Trudy cut her eyes behind Chloe. "And perhaps a side of lanky hunky-ness with that order?" The fifty-something woman laughed.

Chloe blushed. She adored her hometown, but everyone knowing everybody else's business was a definite downside to small-town life.

Trudy winked at her. "The carpenter's right easy on the eyes, isn't he?" She wasn't wrong about Noah. But he'd been oblivious to Chloe that long-ago summer.

She sniffed. "I'm sure I don't know what you mean."

Trudy grinned. "Will this order be to-go?"

Her heart seized. She couldn't do this. She wasn't a brash, push-yourself-forward girl. Not then or now.

"Make it to-go, Trudy."

The peroxide blonde placed the parchment-wrapped piece of pie in a white paper bag. She capped the disposable cup of steaming coffee and handed it to Chloe.

Clutching the coffee cup, she grabbed the bag and rose from the stool.

This was a bad idea. But she needed to make sure the festival opened on schedule. She couldn't let everyone down. Maybe he'd relish the chance to give something back to the community.

Or maybe he'd laugh her right out of the diner.

LaToya, Christopher, the kids in Mrs. Phillips's class and little Lili flashed through her mind. Chloe squared her shoulders.

She couldn't—wouldn't—fail the children of Truelove.

Chapter Two

$\sim$

Sipping his coffee at the diner, Noah sorted through a dozen different possibilities for how he knew the young woman sitting at the counter.

Who'd literally fallen out of the sky and into his arms.

He was sure he didn't know her from Nashville or Los Angeles. She didn't have the over-the-top, over-tanned and over-operated-upon look he'd encountered in most of the women who'd occupied his former life.

Actually, she reminded him of Fliss. Not physically, though. Unlike the woman's long silky locks trailing her shoulder blades, his sister had kept her dark hair pixie short. Also, Fliss's eyes, like his and Lili's, had been blue, not a rich, warm brown.

Too close to quitting time to start painting the gazebo, he'd taken a coffee break to wait for Lili to get out of the after-school program. When the mystery woman strolled into the diner for the second time in less than an hour, his heart had done a sudden, inexplicable uptick.

Lingering over his coffee, he kept a surreptitious watch on the brunette. She wore a white button-down shirt tucked into a pair of jeans and black flats.

Unlike his willowy sister, the cat rescuer was petite. But both women had a natural, outdoorsy appeal. "Outdoorsy" sparked images of an open-air amphitheater, set against a backdrop of jagged mountain peaks.

When the woman with the teasingly familiar face turned

from the counter to walk away, his memory solidified. He knew her from Colorado.

From the summer music festival where he'd first made a name for himself. After his first song went viral, but before he got the call to audition for the nationally broadcast talent show.

Back then, he was a twenty-three-year-old nobody with nothing but driving ambition. The opening act before the well-known evening headliner took the stage. She was the college intern, who'd worked backstage.

It was her turning away that nailed her identity for him. That was what she'd done the entire summer—every time he got within a yard of her. Like a dissonant chord, she'd confused and vexed him.

With everyone else, she'd been as friendly as a puppy dog. With a forthright, open manner. Bubbly with a naive enthusiasm he found strangely endearing. The crew's BFF and go-to gal.

But not his.

For some reason, she hadn't liked him. An unusual experience for him. Females had always liked him. Not that he encouraged it. He'd always found their attention an unwelcome distraction from the only thing that really mattered— the music.

Noah stared into the contents of his mug.

He hadn't played a guitar in public for four years. He was happy being a nobody again. He liked working with his hands. A satisfying, if sometimes lonely, life with only a four-year-old for company.

Yet when she got off the stool, his pulse leaped. She headed for the exit. What *was* her name? Kelly? No, that wasn't right. Carly?

It didn't matter. If she recognized him, it was probably for the best he'd soon finish the gazebo. Time for him and Lili to hit the road again.

At the door, she turned.

Sudden fear hit him like a sledgehammer to the chest. She had the power to destroy everything he'd built in the last few years. Unmask his true identity. Expose him—and Lili—to the fierce glare of public scrutiny.

Keep walking... Don't stop...

The faint trace of honeysuckle heralded her arrival. He jerked his gaze to hers.

"We need to talk, Mr. Knightley."

Chloe set her coffee and the bag on the table.

Those cobalt blue eyes of his cut right through her. The sheer handsomeness of him rattled her, but she reminded herself of her purpose.

She slid into the booth across from him. "I want to thank you for catching me when I fell the other day. You saved my life."

He shrugged. "Hardly."

She leaned forward. "You certainly saved me from injury and allowed me to keep my dignity intact." Though according to the earful she'd received from her brothers post-rescue, the last point was debatable.

He tilted his head. "I don't believe we've met." His trademark crooked smile danced across his features.

Wow. Her nerve endings tingled. Such an effortless charm. She almost faltered in her resolve. But she'd seen the rakish look splashed across too many magazine covers to allow it to sidetrack her.

"I'm Chloe Randolph."

Something akin to recognition dawned in his eyes. "Chloe." He said her name, drawling out the syllables as if trying it on for size. Then the arm's length aloofness he wore like a shield fell over his countenance again. "It's nice to meet you."

"I didn't expect you to remember me though we've met before." She moistened her lips. "But I know you. You're Noah Knightley."

Wariness replaced his guileless look. "My name is Noah Brenden."

"Your name is Knightley. Since our paths crossed at the Colorado music festival, you've racked up an impressive amount of hit singles and awards."

A muscle ticked in his cheek. "You have me confused with someone else." His eyes darkened. "I'm a preservation carpenter here to rebuild the gazebo."

"It's your restoration skills that are of most interest to me now. I'd like to offer you a job."

He crossed his arms over his denim shirt. "I have a job."

"The gazebo project will soon be done." She steepled her hands on the tabletop. "Leaving you free to accept your next project."

His eyebrow cocked.

"I stopped by the square to admire your handiwork. Your craftsmanship is amazing." She threw him a winsome smile. "You'd be perfect for the Lyric Theater renovation."

He unfolded his arms. "Thank you, but no."

"Why not?" She opened her palms. "The project pays top dollar to the artisans restoring the theater."

He reached for his cup. "I make it my business not to linger too long in one spot."

She waited till the cup touched his lips. "So there's less chance of anyone discovering your true identity?"

Choking, he set the cup onto the table with a clatter.

"Your reasons for staying out of the spotlight are your own, Mr. Knightley. But you and I know the truth."

His mouth thinned.

She placed her hands, palms down, on the table. "Please hear me out before you turn down my proposal."

His eyes flicked to hers.

She flushed. "What I mean is, working on the gazebo, I'm sure you've noticed the buzz of activity at the Lyric. The movie theater was a touchstone for generations of locals until it closed fifteen years ago due to declining revenue."

"It happened to movie houses across the country."

She nodded. "In its heyday, the theater was an architectural gem. But it's fallen on hard times."

"There comes a point of no return."

She lifted her chin. "The Lyric just needs some tender, loving care—"

"And a couple million dollars to overhaul it."

She narrowed her eyes. "Money isn't an issue."

He snorted. "Money is always an issue."

With difficulty, she held on to her temper. He was trying to distract her so she'd let him off the hook. But this was too important. Neither she nor the scholarship fund could afford for her to lose her cool.

She took a breath. "The Lyric's first major event is a music festival in June. The bands will be an eclectic mix of musical genres, including some indie acts. The renovation has been underway for over a year. We're on a tight schedule, but we lost our woodworker craftsman to a family emergency today. We need someone to restore the grand staircase to get us to the finish line."

"A tough break." His jaw tightened. "But why should I care?"

"You of all people understand how school boards have slashed funding for the arts in classrooms."

His mouth—a very handsome mouth—twisted. "Why me of all people?"

She leveled her gaze at him. "I've done my homework on you, Mr. Knightley."

"It's Brenden," he growled.

"Over the years, you told multiple interviewers how you grew up in Virginia's southwest corner of the Blue Ridge. Like many of Truelove's kids, without the advantages that come from exposure to the arts. It was only through raw talent and sheer determination you rose to such dizzying heights in the music world."

"You should know better than to believe everything you read." He scrubbed his hand over his face. "The man you have me confused with no longer exists. Why is this project so important to you?" His gaze narrowed. "What's your angle?"

She stiffened. "What makes you think I have an angle?"

"Everybody's got an angle."

She glared at him. "If this is what fame and fortune do to a person, then changing from piano performance to music therapy was the best day's work I ever did."

"The best day's work I ever did was walk away from that world, and that's what I intend to keep doing." He swung out of the booth. "Walk away from you and your job offer."

He threw a handful of cash onto the table. "Enjoy a taste of your own medicine." Turning away, he headed for the exit.

What did that mean? Fury shook her. How dare he walk away from her like she was still that starry-eyed intern.

She leaped up after him. "Noah, wait!"

At her raised voice, heads turned. Conversation momentarily ground to a halt. He yanked the glass door open, sending the bell clattering.

Trudy stepped out from behind the register. "Is everything okay, hon?"

"I'm fine." Or she would be, once she gave the arrogant, guitar-playing singer a piece of her mind.

Dashing onto the sidewalk, she caught a nice view of his

back as he disappeared through the trees across the street into the square.

She overtook him outside the gazebo. "I wasn't done talking to you."

"Too bad." He threw a hammer into the toolbox. It made a loud clang. "Because I was done talking to you."

"If you would just hear me out." She set her cup and bag on a step. "I assure you my only *angle* is the children."

He chucked tools into the metal box.

She leveled a look at him. "The arts center is designed to be a flex-use space that will serve not only as an entertainment venue, but a training ground for the children I work with every day. Art and music studios will occupy the second story of the building. The festival will fund a scholarship for the kids."

Moving around the gazebo, he continued tidying the jobsite.

Chloe gritted her teeth. "I need your help, Noah. Without you, the center doesn't stand a chance of opening in time for the festival."

Straightening, he folded his arms across his chest. Against her will, her gaze followed the ripple of muscle under his shirt.

He scowled. "I'm not sticking around this one-stoplight town."

"There are two stoplights in Truelove."

No one dissed her town. Not even the formerly great Noah Knightley.

"There's nothing you could possibly say to convince me to stay one minute longer than I have to in this *two*-stoplight town."

"Not even to make sure no one learns your real name is actually Knightley?" As soon as the words left her mouth, she wished she could recall them.

He stiffened. "Are you blackmailing me?"

"I'd prefer to think of it as an exchange of services."

"And if I don't agree to finish the theater project..." His voice had gone quiet. "You'll alert the media and blow my cover?"

Chloe was more a carrot-versus-stick, honey-versus-vinegar type of person, but she'd come this far. It was too late to turn back now.

"Do the renovation, and you'll have nothing to fear from me."

Noah glared. "Congratulations on mastering the art of coercion. You certainly had me fooled that summer. Here I was thinking how different you were from the others." His eyes glinted. "My mistake."

She handed him a business card. "Tomorrow morning, I'd like to walk you through the Lyric."

He crammed the card into his pocket. He was angry with her and for good reason. The accusation on his face wasn't as hard to bear as the disappointment in his eyes when he looked at her.

"Miss Randolph! Miss Randolph!"

At the sound of the child's voice, they turned.

Everything about him gentled. "Lili-bell." He raised his hand.

At the far edge of the square, accompanied by ErmaJean, Lili Brenden waved.

Breath hitching, Chloe's gaze ping-ponged between him and the little girl. Suddenly, the pieces fell into place. Her new student was Noah's daughter?

Rushing forward, Lili threw her arms around Chloe's waist. "Miss Randolph!"

In a colorful pink pantsuit, ErmaJean joined them. "Noah. Chloe."

He touched Lili's shoulder. "You know Miss Randolph?"

"She's my music teacher. My favorite teacher."

His gaze cut to Chloe. "Is that so?"

A sinking, dreadful feeling settled in her gut.

The older woman glanced between them. "Is everything all right?"

"Everything's fine," Chloe whispered.

"Never better," Noah muttered in a hard, clipped voice.

ErmaJean arched her eyebrow. "See you tomorrow, Lili."

"Bye, Miss ErmaJean."

The three of them watched until the Double Name Club member crossed the street to her car in the school parking lot.

Noah pulled Lili close. "Don't let us keep you from your evening, Chloe."

In other words, get lost.

He crouched next to his daughter. "I want to hear about your day."

This wasn't what Chloe wanted. Although, at the moment, she wasn't sure what she did want. His animosity left her feeling sad. Alone. And lost.

Shoulders slumped, she headed to her car. She hadn't intended for what had started as a legitimate job offer to escalate to blackmail.

Thoroughly ashamed of her behavior, she slumped against the car. There was no way she'd ever rat him out to the news media, especially after realizing Lili was his daughter.

He must have his reasons for putting his former life behind him. Reasons that were none of her business. A lot was riding on the completion of the renovation. Tears stung her eyes. Yet how could she justify the good the center would do the children if Lili was hurt in the process?

She swiped the moisture from her face. She'd apologize to Noah Knightley, or whatever he called himself, rescind her demands and assure him she'd never breathe a word of his true identity. Thanks to her, he probably couldn't wait to leave Truelove behind in a cloud of sawdust with Lili.

The idea of never seeing him or Lili again made her sadder than she would have imagined.

Tidying the jobsite, Noah kept his eye on Lili. Per her usual afternoon routine, she went looking for the pesky Felix.

He also kept watch on Chloe Randolph. Stopping beside a navy blue SUV, she just stood there and stared at the pavement.

Noah took a quick survey of the gazebo. If he did say so himself, he'd done good work. Granddad, who'd taught him everything he knew about woodworking, would have been proud.

Tomorrow he'd put a final coat of paint on the structure. He grimaced. After his command performance at the Lyric with Chloe.

"Stay where I can see you," he called to Lili.

Flashing him a sweet smile—so like Fliss it cut him to the quick—she hummed a song.

Lili loved music. One of the few things—besides the stray cat—that brought the shy little girl out of her shell.

She'd only been in school a few days when the director approached him about Lili's social awkwardness. They never stayed in one place long enough for her to make friends.

The director had suggested Lili take part in a Very Young Musicians class, designed for preschoolers who found interactions with other children difficult.

He'd seen an immediate difference. Lili raved about her music teacher, the kid-size instruments, the songs and games.

Miss Randolph, as it turned out, was his Chloe Randolph. He rubbed the back of his neck. Not his. Just a girl he'd known a lifetime ago.

At the sound of gravel crunching underfoot, his head snapped up. Her. Again.

"What do you want now?"

Chloe's mouth trembled. "I-I came to apologize."

"You can save your apologies for someone who—"

"And to release you from the project."

That silenced him.

Her dark brown eyes were red rimmed. Had she been crying? For reasons he preferred not to examine, her tears unsettled him. But considering the way things had gone down between them, he hardened his heart. "Why the sudden about-face?"

Chloe gazed at him, misery etched across the gentle planes of her face. "Our conversation escalated in a way I hadn't planned. I would never reveal your real identity. Even before I realized Lili was your daughter."

Something squeezed inside his chest. "Lili isn't—"

"It was wrong of me to threaten you. Terribly wrong." She locked eyes with him. "You have no reason to take me at my word, but I promise your secret is safe with me."

Despite his mistrust of humankind in general, he found himself believing her. Or maybe he was at a point where he wanted—desperately needed—to believe in someone, in something.

She knotted her hands. "I have no right to ask for your forgiveness, but I do anyway. Sincerely."

"What about the renovation?"

"Not your problem." She turned. "I won't bother you anymore."

"Wait…" He touched her arm.

Sparks shot from his fingertips to his forearm. Her eyes widened. She'd felt it too?

"Felix!" Lili screamed. "No, no, no!"

His heart jackhammering, he swung around. Lili lay on the cold, pebbly path beside a bench. He raced forward with Chloe at his heels.

Noah sank to the ground. "Are you hurt? Talk to me, Lil." He pulled her into his lap.

Chloe went down on her knees beside them. "What's happened?"

"He's dead," Lili sobbed. "I killed him like I killed my mother." She buried her face in her small hands.

Chloe sucked in a breath.

The ache in his chest intensified. "That isn't true, Lili." Catching her chin between his thumb and forefinger, he lifted her face. "It's not your fault your mom died. And it's not your fault the cat—"

"Felix isn't dead." Chloe pointed under the bench. "His chest moved. He's breathing."

"You have to do something, Noah." Lili shook him. "Don't let Felix die."

A helpless feeling consumed him. What could he do? He was going to fail her. Again.

"My friend Ingrid is a veterinarian." Chloe sat back on her heels. "Her office is a few blocks down Main Street. I can take Felix to her."

Lili tilted her head. "What's a better-narian?"

Her teacher smiled. "A veterinarian is an animal doctor."

"Can she fix Felix?"

Noah threw Chloe a warning glance. *Don't promise what you can't deliver.*

"She's an excellent animal doctor," Chloe assured Lili. "There's nobody better to take care of Felix."

Lili nodded. "Okay."

Rising, Chloe brushed the gravel off the knees of her jeans. "I'll get a blanket from my car to transport Felix to the clinic."

He moved Lili out of his lap. "We'll follow you there."

"But Noah…" Lili tugged at his sleeve. "Felix is scared to ride by himself to the better-narian."

"Lili is welcome to ride in my car and hold Felix." Chloe

tucked a strand of hair behind her ear. "I have a child's booster seat already secured in the back seat. For my nephew."

Lili pulled at his arm. "Please, Noah...please."

Chloe looked at him. "Please, Noah."

No way he could resist the both of them.

"Sure. Whatever."

Lili flung her arms around his waist. Chloe smiled. A smile that had a curious effect on his resolve to dislike her.

He carefully removed the cat from underneath the bench. Felix's swollen eyelids fluttered before shutting again. The stray didn't look good.

Noah followed Chloe and Lili in his truck. The journey to the vet clinic was mercifully brief. He carried the fleece-wrapped stray into the office. The vet met them at the check-in desk.

"Thank you for seeing us right away, Ingrid." Chloe wrung her hands. "I mean, Dr. Abernathy."

Ingrid Abernathy was a strikingly attractive, cool blonde with a brisk, competent air. "Who do we have here?"

"This is Noah Kni—" Chloe swallowed. "Noah and Lili Brenden."

Lying didn't come easily to Chloe Randolph. Good to know.

"I meant who is my patient?" Brushing them aside, the vet frowned. "Lay him here please."

Noah deposited the cat on a small gurney. Lili maintained a death grip on his hand. "This is Felix."

The vet listened to the cat's chest and lungs.

Dr. Abernathy straightened, letting the stethoscope drape around the collar of her lab coat. "Nasal congestion. Lethargy." The vet ran her gaze over the cat. "I'm guessing a fever, too. Have you noted a loss of appetite?"

He shrugged. "Felix is a stray."

The vet's gaze snapped to his. "Who's going to be responsible for the medical costs?"

Chloe's dark eyes flashed. "I'll cover the costs, Ingrid."

"No, you won't." He stepped in front of Lili's teacher. "I will."

"Fill out the paperwork." Dr. Abernathy handed him a clipboard. "I think we're dealing with a URI."

Lili placed her hand over her mouth.

Chloe put her arm around Lili. "What's a URI?"

"Upper respiratory infection."

He stared at the vet. "The cat has a cold?"

Abernathy gave him a steely look. "Severe infections can lead to blindness."

Lili whimpered.

Chloe glared at her vet friend. "But with Dr. Abernathy's expert care, it won't come to that, will it, Ingrid?"

"I'll know more after a full examination." The vet motioned toward the reception room. "I'll return as soon as I can." Dr. Abernathy wheeled the gurney through a double set of doors.

Lili pulled at him. "What can we do, Noah?"

"The best thing of all, Lili-bell." He squeezed her hand. "We can pray for Felix, right?"

Chloe threw him a startled look.

The wild, bad-boy image he'd cultivated hadn't been just for show. But Noah Brenden was different from the other Noah.

He led them to a pair of upholstered chairs. Lili clambered into Chloe's lap, tucking her head under Chloe's chin. Within seconds, he detected the soft sound of her breathing.

"She's asleep," Chloe whispered.

He rubbed the kinks from his neck. "The vet's bedside manner leaves much to be desired."

Chloe sighed. "She's better with animals than she is with people."

He shook his head. "Good news for Felix."

A smile tilted at her lips. "My friend is a work in progress."

He propped his elbows on the arm rests. "Aren't we all?"

"Despite my best efforts, the blind date with the dairy farmer didn't go as well as I'd hoped."

He blinked. "What?"

She gave him the scoop on the Double Name Club and their extracurricular activities.

"They're also known as the Truelove Matchmakers." She stuck her tongue in her cheek. "I figured you'd appreciate the pseudonym."

He snorted.

She grinned. "Too soon?"

It was hard staying mad at someone like Chloe.

Her smile faded. "What Lili said about her mother..."

"Fliss had epilepsy her entire life, but with proper medication, she'd turned a corner. A few hours after Lili's birth, the seizure caught everyone off guard. The doctors weren't able to save her."

Compassion shone from Chloe's features. "I'm so sorry. How terrible for you and the child she never got to know."

He scrubbed his face with his hand. "I don't understand where Lili got the notion she killed Fliss."

"Children think deeper thoughts than we give them credit for. What about Lili? Is her health okay or does she—"

"No, she doesn't have epilepsy."

Chloe brushed her cheek against Lili's hair. "I'm glad."

Her gesture was so sweet it momentarily robbed him of breath. This was the Chloe Randolph he remembered. Not the woman who'd tried to strong-arm him into doing the renovation.

Everyone had moments they weren't proud of. He'd had entire years he wasn't proud of. Who was he to hold a grudge?

The vet returned to the waiting room. Rubbing her eyes, Lili reached for Noah. He took her in his arms. He could feel the fierce pounding of her heart underneath her cotton dress.

"It's okay," he whispered, stroking her back. "Noah's here."

"A URI." The vet stuck her hands in her lab coat pockets. "Felix's virus will need to run its course. Treatment should be focused on alleviating symptoms, restorative care and rest."

She went on to prescribe an eye ointment and lots of fluid to reduce the chance of dehydration. "He should make a full recovery."

Lili's blue eyes gleamed. "That's why you're a better-narian. You make animals better."

The permafrost in the veterinarian's eyes softened. "Exactly." She turned to Noah. "The vet tech will bring him out in a moment."

His gut clenched. "The motel has a no-pet policy."

Chloe crouched beside his niece. "Would it be okay if I took Felix to my house for the next few days? You can visit him anytime you want."

He shook his head. "I couldn't ask you—"

"You're not asking. What do you think, Lili?"

His niece caught her bottom lip between her teeth. "Will it be okay with your mommy and daddy for Felix to sleep over?"

Chloe's eyes flitted to his and back to Lili. "Totally fine. It's only me and my brother."

"Thank you, Dr. Abernathy." He shook her hand. "I'll settle the bill at the desk."

Minutes later, the tech came out with Felix inside a cat carrier.

Dr. Abernathy walked them to the door. "I added the carrier to your bill."

Of course, she had.

At Chloe's car, he secured the carrier on the back seat. Lili climbed inside to tell the cat good-night.

"Thank you, Chloe." He leaned against the car. "For everything."

She hung on to the driver-side door. "You're welcome."

Chloe had been so kind to Lili. She was so attached to her teacher, to the cat, to Truelove.

Noah stuffed his hands in his pockets. "If it's okay with you, I'd like to finish the staircase at the Lyric."

Her eyes widened. "Do you mean it? Would you?"

Noah shuffled his feet. "If you still want me."

"I still want you."

Their gazes locked.

His heart skipped a beat. She blushed. In his former life, he hadn't realized there were women who still possessed the capacity to blush.

"Are you sure?"

"Lili can finish out the school year." He shrugged, aiming for a nonchalance he was far from feeling. "I'm sure."

"Thank you."

He cocked his head at Chloe. "Nine sharp."

She smiled. "Nine sharp."

For a host of reasons, staying in Truelove was probably a bad idea. But as he and Lili got into his truck, he couldn't think of a place on earth he'd rather be.

Chapter Three

The next morning, Noah hurried Lili into her preschool class.

It was a bright, cheerful room with crayon-colored, child-size furniture. Other children were already engaged in various play stations.

Working in the square every day, he liked to imagine Lili having fun with the other kids. She wasn't having much fun now, though. Brow puckered, she'd once again glued herself to his side.

Lili was tired. He was tired. Breakfast had been a banana and carton of milk in the truck on the way to Truelove. Not an auspicious start for either of them.

He put his hand on her small shoulder. "Don't you want to play with your friends?"

Braids flying, she shook her head, but the longing with which she surveyed her classmates spoke volumes. She wanted very much to have friends. She just didn't know how to bridge the gap from outsider to belonging.

Her teacher left several little girls at the costume box and came over to greet them.

The forty-something woman smoothed a hand over Lili's head. "Are you having a hard morning, sweetheart?"

He stuck his hands in his pockets. "It's my fault. Lili didn't get to bed until late."

After leaving Felix in Chloe's capable hands, it had been a restless night for them both at the motel.

The teacher touched the child's cheek. "Would you put

your backpack in your cubby? That's what we do first thing when we get to school every morning."

Noah helped Lili slip out of the princess pink backpack and handed it to her. Lili gave him an anxious look.

He threw her a smile. "Go ahead."

Lili moved toward her cubby.

"She's made so much progress. I'd hate to see her retreat into her shell, Mr. Brenden." Her teacher patted his arm. "Today is probably just a temporary setback."

Lili returned to his side and recaptured his hand. A minor squabble broke out among the little girls.

"If you'll excuse me a second..." The teacher headed toward the girls.

Praying for a breakthrough, he nudged his chin at a young, blond boy in a colorful plastic smock dabbing paint with broad brushstrokes on a large, blank sheet of paper set on an easel. "Who's that, Lili-bell?"

"Parker is Miss ErmaJean's great son."

Great-grandson?

Parker waved at Lili. She gave him a shy wave in return.

Suddenly Noah became aware of another little boy standing at his elbow.

"Hey, Lili."

"Hey, Jeremiah."

"Wanna play grocery store?" The child looked at Lili. "You can use the scanner, and I'll put the groceries in the bag."

Noah cocked his head. "A scanner?"

A pleased smile curved her small lips. "It beeps."

"Cool."

Jeremiah made as if to move away. "You wanna play with me, Lili?"

She let go of Noah's hand. "Okay."

He was breathing a sigh of relief when she snagged hold of

his shirt sleeve. "We'll go see Felix after school? You didn't forget, did you?"

"I haven't forgotten."

Apparently, he and Chloe Randolph were destined to spend most of the day together.

The little boy said something to Lili, and she laughed as they piled plastic fruit into a pint-size cart.

He eased the classroom door shut behind him. This was exactly what he and the teacher had been working toward— for Lili to gain enough self-confidence to interact with the other kids. But becoming second fiddle to a cat and her play-mates was going to require getting used to.

Exiting the building, he cut across the square toward the arts center.

How boring was he that his entire world revolved around a four-year-old? Noah used to be a fun guy. He marched past the gazebo. He was still a fun guy.

Touring with the band, his fun had mainly consisted of hard liquor, fast cars and women. But those days were over. He never wanted to be that Noah again.

What he needed was a hobby.

He crossed the street. Dodging the scaffolding where work-men in hard hats worked on the old Hollywood-style movie marquee, he took the broad, granite steps two at a time. He reached for the shiny brass handle of the glass door.

Truelove was surrounded by several state and national parks. Why not take advantage of his surroundings to do some hiking?

He stepped into the cavernous theater lobby. "Whoa."

The marble floor was laid out in a series of interlock-ing black and white tiles in a geometric design. Perched on a ladder, a woman was painstakingly re-gilding elaborate plasterwork on the wall. A crew installed a massive, ornate crystal chandelier.

"It's amazing, isn't it?"

His pulse did a strange staccato step.

Chloe had gathered her long dark tresses off her neck and clipped her hair into a messy bun. "It's called a wedding-cake chandelier."

He nodded. "Because it looks like an upside-down wedding cake."

"Thankfully none of the Austrian crystals had been broken. The lighting design team had only to rewire and refresh it. It's one of the three that originally graced the lobby of the Lyric when it opened in 1914."

Chloe wore an oversize blue shirt and a white tank top over faded blue jeans. "Back in the day, the Lyric was the showpiece of the county. The great vaudeville acts performed here. Later in the 1920s, a timber baron modernized the theater into a movie palace. During the world wars, the troop trains ran soldiers from training camps farther south to troop ships in New York harbor headed for Europe. The Truelove Women's League ran a stopover canteen for them in the Lyric."

Noah cocked his head. "You really get into the history of this place, don't you?"

Her eyes sparkled. "Can't you just imagine doughboys and GIs finding true love with their sweethearts?"

"You're a romantic."

She propped her hands on her hips. "You say that like it's a bad thing. Aren't poets like you romantic, too?"

"I'm not a poet."

"Songwriting is poetry set to music."

"I gave people what they wanted. It was a business strategy." He shrugged. "I don't write songs anymore. I'm a carpenter. The sooner I finish the job, the sooner I can shake the dust of Truelove off my feet."

Her eyes flashed. "You can be such a jerk."

"You're just figuring that out? Why do you think I steered clear of you in Colorado?"

She reared a fraction. "What?"

"Forget it."

He moved toward the sweeping staircase. It didn't take much imagination to see how grand and opulent the staircase—the entire theater—had once been. Not that he'd admit that to Chloe Randolph. Standing back, he assessed the project before him.

A trace of honeysuckle wafted past his nostrils. A bead of sweat broke out on his brow. He had a sneaking suspicion prolonged proximity to honeysuckle could be his undoing.

"How about we start with a tour?"

"Sure." He eyed a particularly exquisite rosette carved into one of the newel posts. "An overview would give me the scope of the restoration."

"Let's save the staircase for last." She led him down the length of the lobby. "Phase one involved a complete overhaul of the guts of the building. The sound engineers finished their work last week. The committee's goal has been to restore as much of the original elements as possible while also modernizing them. Including putting in more bathrooms." She flung open a heavy, soundproof door.

Passing into the auditorium, he inhaled sharply. New life had been breathed into the palatial crimson-and-gold theater of a bygone era. The plush, velvety seats sloped amphitheater style to a large stage and a massive red curtain.

"I'm impressed."

She smiled. "A high compliment from someone who's performed at the Grand Ole Opry."

He frowned.

She gestured. "The silent films included live piano music. The orchestra pit has been updated and the backstage area expanded."

He fingered his chin. "A beautiful venue for live performances."

"The engineers also installed a state-of-the-art projector. We plan to show family-friendly films and host a kids' discount movie club once a week during the summer with old-fashioned prices. Two-dollar movie tickets with snacks and a drink included. I have fond memories of coming here each week during summer vacation with my brothers."

He did a slow three-sixty of the place. "The movie theater near my grandparents' farm had the same kind of deal during the summer. My sister and I looked forward to it every week." He shrugged. "Not much for teenagers to do except…" He grimaced. "Get into trouble."

"Same in Truelove. It was actually our police chief's idea to bring back the summer movie club. Good, clean fun. Provide an alternative to less savory temptations."

They wandered into the lobby again. At the refurbished concession stand, she introduced him to the project manager, Colton Atkinson, from Drake Construction.

"You should've seen the state of this place when we started the renovation, but it's coming together." Colton chuckled. "I can almost smell the popcorn."

"I'm giving Noah the grand tour."

"After you're done, Noah, there'll be paperwork to fill out regarding the usual contract liability issues. I could also show you a collection of historic photos, if you'd be interested."

"I'd like that." He gazed at the marbled foyer. "This is fascinating."

The project manager grinned. "We'll make a true believer out of him yet, won't we, Chloe?"

She steered Noah toward the grand staircase.

"Colton seems like a great guy." Noah pursed his lips. "There's something about him… Former military?"

"Truelove's own hometown hero." She sighed. "His proposal to his childhood sweetheart, Mollie, was the most romantic thing I've ever seen in my life."

Noah cut his eyes at her. "You are a hopeless romantic."

Her mouth flattened. "And you don't have a romantic bone in your body, do you?"

"Nope."

"I can't figure out how you managed to write a song as gushingly romantic as 'Sweet Tea, Cutoff Jeans and Flip-Flops' yet remain so cynical."

His gaze darted. "Shout it to the world, why don't you?"

"Paranoid much, Brenden?"

"Naive much, Randolph? I've seen people sell out their own mothers for a few bucks from the paparazzi."

She shook her head. "This is Truelove, not LA."

"When it comes to cold hard cash, no need to test folks beyond what they are able."

"You may be the most antisocial person I've ever known." She fluttered her hand. "But your secret is safe with me."

"I'm holding you to that."

She bit her lip. "The Lyric is more than merely a renovation. This piece of history is important to Truelove's future. Often when a historic theater is revitalized, the entire community is revitalized, too. People won't have to leave home to find jobs."

"You're assuming people want to find a way to stay in this *two*-stoplight town."

She bristled. "Truelove is a great place to call home."

Didn't take much to wind her up about her beloved hometown. Only problem was, Chloe Randolph became even more attractive the more animated she got. Which had a curious effect on his determination to keep her at arm's length.

"I think your memories of home and mine differ." He removed his phone from his pocket to take a few photos for later reference. "Probably should get a look at the staircase. I've also a gazebo to finish before this day is over."

"Fine." She threw out her hands. "I'll get off my soapbox."

He focused on the project. The sweeping staircase was a double stringer with carved wooden balusters on both sides. His gaze roamed up the split staircase to the two small, narrow jut-outs on either side of the V, overlooking the foyer below.

"Juliet balconies," he grunted.

"Soooo romantic."

He made notes on his phone. "I'll grant you a place like this requires a certain level of drama."

"You don't believe in love?"

"No, I do not. The Juliet balcony railings will have to be hand-scraped." Bending, he took a close shot of one of the intact balusters. "I'm counting ten that are cracked and will need to be repaired or recreated."

He moved up the staircase, taking inventory of what needed to be done.

She trailed after him. "If you don't believe in love, what *do* you believe in?"

"Lili." Crouching on the landing, he pointed. "Some chump had the less than stellar idea to slap a coat of paint on the stairs."

"Utter sacrilege."

"Totally." His mouth twitched. "Then to add insult to injury, he spread a layer of polyurethane on top."

"So wrong."

"On so many levels." He cocked his head. "The latex over the oil paint is flaking. The landing will need to be refinished. The risers need a good scrub. Lots of staple holes to fill. The treads will need to be sealed, too." He rose.

"So you're telling me you have a lot of work ahead of you."

He gave the handrailing a small shake. It wobbled. "I'm

telling you historical preservation is wonderful, but safety is more important. This is unstable and no longer meets current safety codes."

She sank onto the step. "Oh."

Her distress tugged at his heartstrings. "The safety protocols have to be met, but that doesn't mean historical preservation has to be scrapped. With a few adjustments to the original design, I think no one but a diehard like you will notice the difference."

"You can do this?"

"I can."

"Before the festival opens?" She moistened her bottom lip. "It sounds like an enormous amount of work."

"It is an enormous amount of work. But yeah, I think I can make it happen by the deadline." He made a face. "I keep most of my tools and equipment in a portable trailer I pull behind my truck, but for something this extensive... The work would go faster if I had some place to set up shop."

"I might have the perfect solution." She smiled. "I'll need to reach out to a few people first, though."

Noah offered her his hand. She placed her hand in his, and he pulled her to her feet.

Her fingers were strong and straight. He would have expected no less from a person who spent copious amounts of time playing the piano. What he didn't expect was the electric charge that went from her hand against his skin, straight up his arm.

The last thing he needed was to get involved with Chloe Randolph. With his track record, he'd be doing her a favor to stay far, far away.

Pulling free, she tucked a strand of hair behind her ear. He followed the movement of her hand. His heart thudded in his chest. The sooner he finished this job, the better for everyone.

He cleared his throat. "I'd best get to work."

"Do you and Lili still plan to stop by this afternoon to visit Felix?"

He glanced over his shoulder at her. "If it's okay with you. Lili is looking forward to seeing Felix."

"I'm looking forward to seeing Lili."

But not him. Theirs was a professional relationship, he reminded himself for the umpteenth time this morning. Shouldn't be this big of an issue. His middle name was professional.

Actually, his middle name was Ryder.

She resettled her purse strap on her shoulder. "Four thirty?"

Nodding, he shoved his hands into his jeans pockets. He looked at her. She looked at him. Neither of them moved.

At a sudden clatter from the foyer, they jolted.

"I'll text you my address." She fingered the purse strap. "I should get going. Places to go. Students to teach."

"Me, too." He shook his head. "Not school. The gazebo." He grimaced.

What was it about Chloe Randolph that reduced him to monosyllables? He used to write chart-topping ballads. With an effort, he wrenched his gaze away and turned on his heel. *Keep it professional, dude.*

It was one of those days. Chloe dashed from one school to the next. From one student session to the other.

Her life would slow down once the renovation was complete. Once the arts center opened. After the music festival…

Of course, after the project was complete, Noah and Lili would have long since moved on from Truelove. Frowning, she pulled into her driveway.

Slinging her music bag with case notes over her shoulder, she got out of the car. Noah and Lili would be here soon. She was nearly to the door when her brother's splashy red convertible pulled into the driveway.

He joined her on the porch. "What's going on, Chlo?"

"I explained in the text—"

"Why would you imagine I'd be fine with you opening our family home to a stranger?"

"He's not—" She pressed her lips together. "Alan and Travis are fine with letting the Brendens stay in the loft apartment above Dad's old workshop until the Lyric is finished."

Her brother jutted his jaw. "I don't have time to deal with another one of your harebrained schemes."

Chloe was sick of his eldest-sibling superiority. He treated her like she didn't have the good sense God gave small animals. But Jeffrey treated most people like they were one key short of a full chord. He was somebody important at the local bank, and he never let an opportunity pass to let everybody know it.

She crossed her arms. "It's not harebrained. I called Mom and Dad in Florida. They are perfectly fine with this short-term arrangement. The only one not on board, as usual," she paused for effect, "is you."

He glared. "Always leaping before you look. No thought to long-term consequences. Or the optics."

"What optics?"

"A man and my sister living alone here together."

Somebody like Noah would have zero interest in a small-town music therapist like her. She'd followed his career. Judging from publicity photos at various music award shows, tall, exotic and glamorous appeared more his type.

"His daughter will be with him. The workshop loft isn't even connected to the main house. Not that my virtue is in any danger."

"Travis works long hours on shift with the highway patrol. He won't always be around to safeguard your reputation."

"Is it truly my reputation that has you in such a snit, or yours?"

He drew up. "The Randolphs have an image to maintain. A responsibility you've never taken—"

"Noah and Lili are going to live in the apartment over the workshop for the next two months. You can either like it or lump it. Your choice. But it's going to happen."

"I'm only trying to look out for my baby sister."

She snorted. "Shouldn't you be getting back to work? Wouldn't want your absence to trigger a financial crisis."

His mouth thinned. "I'm not happy about this."

"You're not happy about most things."

He rocked on his heels. Jeffrey tended to hide behind an iron mask of competence. Unintentionally, she'd hit a nerve.

"Jeff, I'm sorry—"

"His name is Noah?" A gleam of calculation lanced his dark eyes. "Why does that ring a bell?"

Sudden fear assailed her. They would be here at any moment. Jeffrey needed to be gone before they arrived on the off chance he might recognize Noah. Her brother could be a jerk, but stupid he was not.

Chloe fumbled through her purse for the house key. "Surely you have farms to foreclose on and families to evict?"

"I've never... You have no idea what I do for this town, Chloe." His face reddened. "I'll go, but this conversation isn't over. Not by a long shot."

He stomped toward his car. Seconds later, tires screeching, he roared down the street.

She'd managed a short reprieve. Long enough for Noah and Lili to visit without getting ambushed by Jeffrey.

Inside the house, Felix appeared in the hallway, rubbing against her ankles in feline welcome. At least someone was glad to see her.

Jeffrey was being overprotective. She was a grown woman. She didn't need his protection.

Noah needed a place to do his work. She had the perfect space. It only made sense that having Noah and Lili living in the loft apartment would ensure the project proceeded smoothly.

As for living closer to her? Better for the project. Not so much for her heart.

For the first time, a twinge of trepidation took the edge off her earlier enthusiasm.

Putting away her bag, her hand shook. She was being ridiculous.

Glimpsing his truck turn onto the street, her heart pounded.

Chapter Four

Turning into Chloe's neighborhood, Noah glanced in the rearview mirror. Strapped into her booster seat, Lili gazed out the window. Mature hardwoods formed a canopy of green over the street.

Only five minutes from the north end of Main Street, the subdivision included wide lawns and cute two-story, middle-class homes built in the 1980s with lots of curb appeal. He pulled up to the nautical blue house with the crisp white trim.

"Miss Randolph's on the porch." Lili pointed. "Felix is with her, too."

Chloe must have been on the lookout for them. She waved at Lili. Tail flicking, the feline twined around Chloe's ankles. Quite the welcoming committee.

A thought arose unbidden of how nice it would be to always have someone watching for him. Welcoming him home. Something pinged inside his chest.

He swallowed. This was Chloe's home, not his and Lili's. They didn't have a home.

No sooner had he freed Lili from the truck than she dashed toward her teacher and the tuxedo cat. Chloe caught Lili in a quick hug. The stray meowed.

Chloe threw him a wistful smile. A smile just for him. "Hi."

The smile did funny things to his equilibrium. He leaned against the white railing. "Hey."

He wouldn't have believed the bubbly music therapist had

a shy bone in her body. Probably something to do with his Noah Knightley persona. In those crazy, whirlwind years, women had either gotten knock-kneed bashful around him or aggressively inappropriate.

It bothered him to think she might still view him as that guy. Deep down, he'd never been that guy. Suddenly, it felt imperative she see the real him—Noah Brenden.

He cleared his throat. "How's the cat?"

"Felix seems to be on the mend."

He propped one foot on the step. "Thanks to you."

Lili snuggled against her teacher. "I like your house, Miss Randolph. It's bee-you-tiful."

She rested her hand on Lili's head. "Thank you, sweetheart."

Crouching, Lili stroked Felix's back. The stray purred.

The music therapist pushed open the front door. "Please come inside." Lili and the cat slipped into the house.

Chloe waited for him. "Technically, the house belongs to my parents, but they've retired to Florida and only visit for the holidays. I'm the resident guardian of our childhood home."

"It's a great childhood home." Noah glanced at the haint blue porch ceiling. "Unlike mine. A dingy, smoky tour bus full of drugged-out rock-and-roll musicians, which also included my mother."

Her lips parted. "Oh. I'm sorry. I didn't realize."

Noah dropped his gaze to the gray planks of the porch. "It doesn't matter." He took a gander at the front door. "I especially like this."

"Thanks." She ushered him inside. "I chose the color for the door." Her eyes twinkling, she shut the door behind him. "Not too blinding?"

"It's inviting." He grinned. "Yellow is so you. Warm, sunny and infectiously optimistic. Happy."

The corners of her eyes lifted, fanning out. "This house has always been a happy house."

He suspected she had a great capacity for happiness. For love. But he shook himself. Not going there. Someone like her wasn't meant for someone like him.

She placed her hand on Lili's shoulder. "Could I interest you in a homemade cookie?"

Lili perked. "Yes, please. And for Felix?"

"Dr. Ingrid says cookies aren't good for cats, but you can help me slice a banana and put it in his bowl."

Lili whipped around to him. "Felix has his own bowl, Noah."

"So I hear."

Chloe glanced over her shoulder at him. "I've found a workshop for you. And if you're interested, I have another idea I'd like to run by you."

Oh, he was interested all right. Far more interested in anything concerning Chloe Randolph than he ought to be.

"Any chance of me getting a cookie?" He shuffled his feet. "I listen better when I'm chewing."

She laughed. "I think something could be arranged."

The foyer led to an open concept space along the back of the house. The eating area contained a large oak table and matching chairs. A picture window overlooked the backyard.

Chloe patted the cushion on a stool at the kitchen island. Sweeping the little girl off her feet, amidst much giggles, he settled Lili onto the stool. Chloe peeled a banana and set it on a wooden cutting board in front of Lili. She handed the child a butter knife.

Lili grinned at him. "I'm a cooker like Miss Randolph."

He and Chloe exchanged a smile. "Just like Miss Randolph," he agreed.

Lili focused on slicing the banana into cat-size slices with the concentration of a basketball player at the free throw line.

There was something about Chloe. A wellspring of joy that brought out the best in Lili. That made him wish he was something better than he was.

Chloe handed him a cinnamon-coated, pale golden cookie. He took a bite. "Wow. Thank you. Snickerdoodle?"

Lili looked up. "That's Noah's favorite."

Chloe tilted her head. "Is it? Good to know. I hope it's one of your favorites, too."

Swallowing the last of the cookie, he rested his palm on Lili's silky brown head. "Lil has many favorites."

"I'm done, Miss Randolph."

"Shall we give Felix his treat?"

Lili lifted her arms to him. Plucking her off the stool, he set her on her small, sandaled feet.

Chloe handed her the cutting board. "Felix sleeps in the laundry room. His bowls are there, too."

On the move, Felix streaked ahead.

Carrying the cookie container, Chloe led them toward a room off the kitchen.

"Ooooh, Noah." Lili's eyes shone. "Felix has his own bed."

The outside of the donut-shaped bed was a gray herringbone pattern. The inside was lined with gray shag fur.

He reached for his wallet. "Let me reimburse you."

She waved away his words. "Ingrid let me raid her supply closet at the clinic." She set the cookies on top of the front-loading washer. "We always had a cat when I was growing up. I found the bowls in the attic."

Lili distributed the banana slices into Felix's food bowl. The cat licked her hand. She giggled.

Peeling back the lid, she allowed Lili to grab a cookie. Munching the cookie, Lili returned to her crouch beside Felix's bowl as he polished off the rest of the banana.

Noah leaned his elbow on the dryer. "Thank you for your kindness to Lili." The cat meowed. "And Felix."

She held the container out to him. "Seconds?"

He reached for another one. "Don't mind if I do. It isn't

often Lili and I get homemade cookies. Yet another way I fail her." He made a wry grimace.

She frowned. "Don't do that."

"What?"

"Don't diss yourself. Humility is one thing, but self-denigration is another thing entirely. You've done an amazing job with your little girl. You two have a wonderful relationship. It's clear how much she loves you."

"You think so?"

"I know so." Chloe smiled at him. "She's blessed to have you as her dad."

Dishonesty didn't sit right with him. "Lili isn't—"

"—I think the space would be perfect for your needs. Shall we go take a look?"

He blinked at her. "What?"

"My dad's old workshop." She gestured toward the backyard. "I thought you said cookies helped you listen better."

He'd been too busy mulling over how to correct her misunderstanding of his relationship with Lili to hear what else she'd apparently said to him.

Flinging open an exterior door, she headed into the backyard. "Come on, you two."

The feline bolted for the exit. Lili ran after him. Noah caught up with everyone outside a large, one-bay garage near the rear of the property. A mini-replica of the house, the two-story outbuilding with dormers wasn't visible from the street.

Chloe opened a door on the side of the garage. "You can unload your equipment, set up shop, and you're only a few minutes from the Lyric."

Lili pointed at a small playground set in the opposite corner of the yard. "Can Felix and I go play?"

He shrugged. "If it's okay with Miss Randolph, I guess—"

Lili darted toward the swing set. Felix raced behind her.

He cut a look at Chloe. "Play equipment?"

"For my nephew when he visits." She gestured at the open door. "Take a look."

He stepped into the cavernous space. It took a minute for his eyes to adjust to the semi-darkened interior.

Workbenches lined both sides of the garage. Tools with sundry purposes hung from pegs on the wall. Toward the back, he spotted a set of stairs that led to the second story.

She threw out her hands. "Isn't it perfect?"

"It would also be the cleanest, most organized space I've ever had to work in." He shook his head. "I wouldn't want to mess it up."

"You wouldn't mess it up. The organization is post-Dad. He's not exactly known for his tidiness when he has a project going."

Noah looked around, getting a feel for the place. "What kind of projects?"

"A little bit of this, a little bit of that. Dad went through a chainsaw phase."

He choked a little.

She laughed. "Think less horror movie, more chainsaw carving." Standing beside one of the windows lining the side of the garage, she waved to Lili. "Buster the Bear by the spruce is one of his creations."

Chainsaw carving? The entire Randolph clan sounded eccentric. He was almost afraid to ask. "And after the chainsaw phase?"

"Dad and the boys restored my grandfather's vintage 1968 Dodge Charger."

He whistled under his breath. "Sweet."

"Dad and Mom drove off into the sunset—aka their Florida retirement—in that vehicle. The boys and I also held our weekly band practice in here."

He cocked his head. "I can't picture you in a boy band."

Noah took a quick peek out of the window, checking on Lili's status. Braids flying, she was enjoying the swing set.

Chloe blushed. "It was nothing like your Nashville band. We led worship for the youth group every week."

If she'd followed his career, she probably also knew of several particular bad choices he'd made. How could she not when his life had been splashed across the tabloids?

The music had led to a world of trouble for him and Fliss. Most of which he was deeply ashamed of now.

"What we lacked in talent, we made up for with enthusiasm." She gazed around the empty bay as if reliving a fond memory. "Jeffrey played lead guitar. Alan played bass. Travis was on the rhythm guitar. I played the keyboard and sang vocals."

His eyebrows arched. "That's a lot of brothers."

She rolled her eyes. "Tell me about it. And there was Zach, who played the drums. We've always hung out a lot. He practically lived here in those days."

Was Chloe in a relationship with this Zach person? Everyone knew that in a band the drummer was usually trouble. Noah took an immediate dislike to the former teenage band member.

She pressed a switch on the wall, and the garage door rose. "Would this work for you?"

"What about your brothers?" He motioned toward the house. "Do they all live here, too?"

"Just Travis. Jeffrey was firstborn." She made a face. "And he never lets the rest of us forget it. Alan lives over the mountain in the county seat with his wife, Bekki, and my handsome little nephew. Travis is closest to my age. Jeffrey moved on to bigger and better things." She sniffed.

He got the distinct impression she and her oldest brother weren't the best of pals.

"What do you think?"

"If I mean to finish the project on time, having a workshop close to downtown would be a blessing." He scanned the space. "To be able to unload only once and lock up when I leave at night."

"Here's the other thing." She tucked a strand of hair behind her ear. "How would you feel about staying in the loft apartment upstairs? There's plenty of room. Two bedrooms, a full bath. Kitchen and dining area."

"Chloe…"

She tugged him toward the staircase. "It sounds grander than it is. Just take a look. And keep an open mind."

But her hand in his had driven all rational thought from his brain. He allowed himself to be towed to the top of the stairs.

The loft was a sun-drenched space. The living area and kitchen flowed into one another. He could all too easily imagine himself sinking into the cozy furniture after a long day's work.

Chloe threw open several doors that led to the bedrooms and bath. "I know it's not much." She wrung her hands. "But I'd really like you to consider it before you automatically say no."

She paced restlessly around the coffee table, making him dizzy. "Say yes for the same reason taking over the workshop downstairs makes sense. But also—"

One of her most endearing traits was how she became even more of a chatterbox when she was nervous. Or wanted something really bad. Like him and Lili relocating to the loft? Probably more Lili than him.

"—because you and Lili wouldn't have to stay at the motel. You'd be much more comfortable here. Lili could spend more time with Felix. She could have her own bedroom."

Lili would love a bedroom of her own. He wouldn't mind more privacy, either. But for every good reason to take Chloe up on her offer, there were a dozen more for why this would be a bad idea.

"I can't rent your apartment, Chloe."

Her eyes widened. "I wouldn't expect you to pay rent. I understand how tight your situation is."

That wasn't what he'd meant. "Just because we're living in a motel doesn't mean I'm a charity case."

"Of course not."

She'd worked her way around the coffee table and stood next to him. Close enough he caught subtle whiffs of honeysuckle. As usual, the scent had a totally adverse effect on his ability to concentrate.

"You're already doing me a big favor by tackling the renovation. Please let me do something for you. It would make me happy to have the both of you here. Lili and I could have such fun." She cocked an eye at him. "And if I can sweeten the deal for you, you might find a few more snickerdoodles in your future, too."

Coming from anyone but Chloe, her last remark might have come across as mildly suggestive. Such innuendo, though, would go entirely over her head. She had such a big heart.

As for sweetening the deal? The snickerdoodles were great, but Chloe shouldn't sell herself short. For him, hands down, she was the bigger deal sweetener. Which only solidified how hazardous such a move could prove to his peace of mind.

"Think how good this could be for Lili."

She wasn't wrong. The stable environment—albeit a temporary one—would be good for Lili.

Chloe gave him a winsome smile. "This place could be your home away from home in Truelove."

Except there was no other home waiting for him and Lili.

"We should ask Lili if she'd want to live here."

He knew what Lili would say. She'd be thrilled. A chance to be near her beloved teacher. To have a place for a pet. A chance to have a real home.

A home for Lili. That above every other consideration sealed the deal for him.

"We'll stay."

This would either be the best decision he'd ever made or the worst. Time would tell. "Thank you for offering us your home."

"I promise you won't regret it."

He already regretted it, but this was for Lili. And, he had a hard time saying no to Chloe Randolph.

She opened several cabinets. "Fully equipped. You'll just need to make a grocery run to fill the fridge and pantry. Then you'll have everything you need to make your own meals with Lili." She paused. "You do know how to cook, don't you, or I could—"

"I know how to cook."

Living on the road like they did, had he ever cooked an actual meal for Lili? Probably not. Wouldn't she be surprised when he whipped out an old Brenden family recipe or two.

Something warm ignited in his chest. Real meals. A real home for Lili. Maybe this wasn't the worst idea ever.

He swallowed. "I don't feel comfortable giving back nothing in return. About the money…"

"I'm sure we can work out an alternative way for you to contribute your fair share."

She gazed at him with an utter lack of guile. She was so puppy-dog friendly with a sincere desire to help. Neighbor to neighbor. Very Truelove.

Very Chloe.

How could he refuse such kindness? Something about her appealed to a Noah he kept buried, mostly out of self-preservation. The Noah who wanted to believe people like her existed. That somewhere in the world a place like Truelove existed.

"Noah?" Lili called from downstairs. "Where are you?"

Leaning over the bannister, he gazed down at the small girl for whom he'd do anything, including abandon his career. "Up here, Lil."

Her anxious face peered at him. She liked having him near. He felt the same, but Lili needed to become more self-reliant and independent. She needed to discover her own strengths.

"Felix and I are coming." She pounded up the stairs. Sprinting ahead, Felix reached the top first.

Lili wrapped her arms around his waist. He'd not realized until the nurse placed the baby in his arms that terrible day it was possible to feel as much love as he did for this one small human. His Lili.

He tugged one of her braids. "Miss Randolph has invited us to move into this apartment while I work at the arts center. Would that be okay with you?"

Lili's eyes grew large. "That would be so awesome." She ran over to Chloe, throwing her arms around the music therapist. "Thank you. Thank you. Thank you, Miss Randolph."

Chloe bent over the child, hugging her. "You are so welcome, honey. I'm looking forward to having you and Noah here."

"And Felix," Lili whispered against Chloe's shirt.

Chloe smiled at him from across the room.

His heart did an inexplicable turn in his chest. He mustn't stand in the way of Lili becoming the amazing person God wanted her to be. Living here would be good for her. If not so much for him.

Lili lifted her head. "Where will I sleep?"

He smiled. "You'll have your own bedroom, Lili-bell."

"Oh, Noah." She did that little happy dance she sometimes did on her tiptoes. "Can I see?"

"Right this way, my dear." Chloe and Lili disappeared into the smaller bedroom. After a minute, Chloe emerged alone. "She's planning how to decorate her room."

"I'll tell her not to—"

"Don't you dare spoil her joy. Feel free to make the place your own. The loft doesn't exactly scream sophistication. It's country simple. Kind of innocent." She wrinkled her cute nose at him. "Like me, I guess."

"Trust me when I tell you sophistication is overrated."

Somehow, without him realizing it, they were standing in front of each other. Either she'd taken a step toward him, or he'd bridged the distance between them. He got a whiff of that tantalizing fragrance she wore. Man, honeysuckle was starting to become his all-time favorite scent.

"Nothing wrong with innocence," he rasped. "It should be protected at all costs."

She looked at him. He looked at her. They were so close his breath fluttered a tendril of hair at her ear. His heart sped up. If he were to bend his head slightly...

From the top of the stairs, a man cleared his throat. "I can't tell you how glad I am to hear you say that. Brenden, isn't it?"

She and Noah jumped apart as if they'd been scalded.

Her hand flew to her throat. "Stop sneaking up on people, Travis."

Ah. One of the brothers. Not that he wouldn't have guessed. They had the same dark hair and eyes, but there the resemblance ended. The man in the North Carolina state trooper's black-and-gray uniform was at least four years older than Chloe. Nearer to Noah's age. Her brother must be with the highway patrol.

Noah had always considered himself fit. And tall. Her brother, however, was a mountain of a man.

The state trooper stuck out his hand. "Travis Randolph."

He took his hand. "Noah Brenden. Pleased to meet you."

Travis's gaze drilled holes into Noah. "Long as you and I understand each other, we'll get along just fine." Her brother squeezed his hand.

He was not exactly a lightweight in the strength department, with his hands roughened and calloused from working with wood. Nevertheless, Noah did his best not to wince.

When the state trooper released his grip, Noah resisted the urge to flex his hand to make sure it still worked.

Flouncing out of the bedroom, Lili rejoined them.

"Who have we here?" Removing his regulation hat, Travis took a knee. "I'm Chloe's much wiser brother."

Chloe snorted. "Lili, meet Sergeant Travis Randolph. Troop G, District 1. A legend in his own mind, ladies and gentlemen." But she smiled.

Her brother threw her a teasing grin. Their clear enjoyment of each other reminded Noah of his relationship with Fliss.

The little girl gave him a shy smile. "Could I try on your hat?"

"Why sure, honey." He handed it over, and Lili plopped it on her head. Falling forward over her eyes, it engulfed her.

She giggled. "Look at me, Noah. I look funny, don't I?"

"Very funny."

Travis rose. "Just wanted to stop by and introduce myself."

And establish a few boundaries, which Noah totally respected. He'd have done the same if Fliss had invited some unknown guy into their lives.

Travis retrieved his hat.

Noah tugged Lili against him. "We should check out of the motel and get our stuff before it gets dark."

Travis fitted the hat on his head and adjusted the angle of the brim. "I'm sure we'll be seeing each other around."

Message received, loud and clear. Not that he needed the warning. Because no matter how much Noah had changed, he knew that Chloe was as far out of his league as darkness was from light.

Chapter Five

After her brother left them, Chloe gave Noah the keys to the garage.

He and Lili needed to check out of the motel. She returned to the house.

Standing well back from the bay window in the living room, she watched the red taillights of his truck disappear down the street.

Chloe found it odd Lili called him by his given name, but she wasn't a parent and what did she know—

"What are you doing, sis?"

"For the love of sweet tea…" Hand to her heart, she whirled. "I thought you'd gone."

Her eyes darted to the window. Only then did she notice the patrol vehicle was still parked beside her SUV.

In his favorite leather recliner, hat in his hands, he leaned forward. Had he been there the whole time and she'd been too intent on the Brendens to notice him sitting in the same room?

Travis's eyebrow rose. "Why so jumpy?"

She frowned. "I'm jumpy because you insist on sneaking around."

"I'm trying to make sure you're not making a mistake."

She crossed her arms over her shirt. "I asked you about inviting the Brendens to stay, and you agreed. Second thoughts now are a little too late."

"I shouldn't have agreed without meeting him first. When I walked in, the two of you seemed…"

She lifted her chin. "Seemed like a friend doing another friend a favor?"

"Like something besides friendliness was going on between you."

She could feel the heat rising from beneath her shirt collar. "I don't know what you think you saw, but..." She pressed her lips together. "I'm not sure why you find the Brendens so objectionable."

Travis fingered the brim of his hat. "Lili is a sweetheart, but the thing is, Chlo, I recognize Brenden, or whatever he's calling himself these days."

She froze.

"How could I not when you came home from Colorado with stars in your eyes? You had posters of the guy on the wall. You made that scrapbook of him with magazine clippings."

Her cheeks burned. She hadn't realized the entire family had been aware of her not-so-secret crush on the country music star.

"People don't change their identity unless they're trying to hide something. I don't trust him. I don't want you to get hurt."

"You're making too much of this. I don't know what you thought you saw, but friendship is all there could ever be between us."

"I wish I believed that. But I know you." He pursed his lips. "You think with your heart, not your head. I don't want your heart to get broken."

"Seriously, Noah and me aren't a thing. Were never a thing."

"Yet you've always had feelings for him. Men like him come and go. Truelove isn't the kind of place a man like that will stick around for long."

Her lips trembled. "I'm well aware I'm not the kind of person a man like Noah would stick around for."

"That's not what I said." Travis gripped his hat. "You deserve the kind of guy who has the moon and stars in his eyes when he looks at you. Not a restless wanderer with commitment issues. Those celebrity types are all glitz but no substance."

"You're not telling me anything I'm not already aware of." She gathered her hair off her neck. "I'm a grown woman. Give me credit for a little sense."

"There's a good guy out there for you, Chlo. I'm sure of it. God has beautiful plans for your life."

"I'm not looking to get into a relationship with anyone. I've got my students. My focus is also on getting the arts center finished and setting up the scholarships." She secured her hair into a ponytail clip. "I've got no time for romance."

"I've watched you do this your entire life, Chloe. You give and give to other people. And what do you have to show for it?"

She propped her hands on her hips. "I don't give expecting anything in return."

"But people take advantage of you. And then you get hurt." He squared his shoulders. "Jeffrey isn't wrong when he says you're too involved in other people's lives and not enough in your own."

Her nostrils flared. "When you two get your own girls is when I'll start taking romantic advice from my brothers."

"We're busy with our careers right now, Chloe."

"So am I. It just happens that part of my career goals includes helping my friends find their own true loves."

"Leave me out of your machinations." He raked his hand over his close-cropped hair. "You're going to do what you want to do no matter what I say, but I'm asking you to be careful. Please don't get too attached to him or Lili. By summer, they'll be gone."

A fact she was only too well aware of.

She clasped her hands under her chin. "You won't tell anyone about Noah's former identity, will you? He left that world behind for his daughter's sake."

Travis's brow furrowed. "If that's true, it's a noble reason. I won't out him, but I won't stand by and let him wreck your life, either."

"If you'd get to know him, you'd see Noah's a good guy."

He clamped his hat on his head. "Maybe I will."

She touched his sleeve. "I appreciate you looking out for me, but I'll be fine. You'll see."

"I hope you're right."

So did she. Oh, so did she.

With Travis on night shift this week, Chloe was once again on her own for supper.

Everyone knew it was easier to cook for more than one person. So she made two plates of her mom's manicotti for Lili and Noah. She left the food on the counter in the garage loft with a quick note wishing them a good night.

Afterward, she worked on a few lesson plans and adjusted her session goals accordingly. But as dusk settled into darkness, she kept an eye out for their return.

She also second-guessed—agonized over—leaving the food. Had she overstepped? Would he regret moving into the garage apartment?

Chloe let her face fall into her hands. She'd done it again, hadn't she? Leaped before she thought things through. Her brothers were right. Noah would think she was an interfering busybody. The food had been too much. *She* was too much.

She'd go over there right now before they returned and retrieve the food. No one would be the wiser to her ill-advised attempt at hospitality. She jumped out of her chair.

Then a beam of headlights swept across the driveway. She groaned.

Too late.

She drifted to the kitchen window. Noah and Lili went into the garage. Seconds later, a light came on upstairs. Full of regrets, she wrung her hands, imagining the worst as he discovered the food she'd left for them.

This sneaking around her own house, watching out the window thing was so middle school. How humiliating if Travis were to catch her mooning over the former country music crooner turned carpenter dad?

Noah's face appeared in the loft window. Her breath caught. Heat flooded her face.

Ducking for cover, she squatted beside the sink cabinet. Her heart pounded. Why hadn't she turned out the light first? Or better yet, given him a "happened to be looking at you same time you're looking at me" wave?

Instead, she'd panicked. He must think she was certifiable. And he'd be right.

She crab-walked her way past the island and into the hallway. No longer in his sightline, she pressed her shoulder blades against the wall. Fanning her face, she rose.

Pull yourself together. Stop being so ridiculous. After the cat in the tree incident, if he ever doubted she was not quite right in the head, he would doubt no more.

Nothing to be done about it now, though. Wasn't like Noah would have ever been interested in her. Not that she wanted him to be interested in her.

Yeah, right. Whatever helps you sleep at night. Not that sleep came easily.

In the early hours of the morning, she heard the faint sound of the latch on the front door. She squinted at the bedside clock. Travis would go to bed and sleep until noon. Satisfied he was safely home, she fell into a deeper slumber.

This time of year, the sun rose early and so did she. Not wanting to disturb her brother, she slipped out of her bedroom.

She spared a glance down the hallway at his closed bedroom door. That was their signal when he was on night shift.

She'd leave it ajar, and he closed it when he returned. Night shift weeks were the worst. She was always glad when he rotated back to day shift.

Chloe tiptoed downstairs.

After Travis became a law enforcement officer, Mom said she never rested well until he was home again. Once her mother left Truelove, Chloe had taken up the baton of looking out for her brother. Like him looking out for her in regard to Noah?

Biting her lip, she measured grounds into the coffeemaker. She wasn't as naive as everyone believed. Noah wasn't the marrying kind. And she could take care of her own heart, thank you very much.

When the coffee was ready, she poured a cup. Across the lawn, the side door to the garage opened. Felix scampered out with Lili not far behind. The little girl hastened toward the play set. No doubt Noah would follow along soon.

Not wishing to repeat last night's cringeworthy episode of being caught staring, she gave the window a wide berth and settled with her cup in her favorite comfy chair in the family room, which overlooked the opposite end of the yard. She loved the splendor of a Blue Ridge spring. The pink-tipped azaleas were almost ready to burst into bloom against the wooden fence.

Savoring the nutty aroma of the coffee, she closed her eyes. The weekdays were so hectic, it felt nice to relax, listen to the chirping of the birds and enjoy the dappled sunshine on her face.

At a loud knock on the kitchen door, her eyes flew open. She jerked, sloshing the coffee and nearly spilling all its contents on her blouse.

Of all the clumsy… Plucking tissues from the box on the

side table, she dabbed at the drops dribbling down the side of the mug.

The knock sounded again.

"Coming!" she shouted before remembering Travis was sleeping.

Scrambling out of the chair, she hurried toward the door. "Hold on." She placed the mug on the counter. "Just a sec—" Twisting the knob, she flung open the door.

Noah took a step back. His gaze pinged from the soggy tissues she still clutched to her face. "I didn't mean to interrupt."

Why did she always look so not-put-together around him?

She sighed. "I was in the middle of spilling my coffee. No biggie." She deposited the fistfuls of tissues on the nearest available surface.

"Is this a recurring problem for you?"

She blew out a breath. "More often than I care to admit."

His very handsome mouth quirked. He handed her the now clean plates she'd left in the loft last night. "I wanted to return these and—"

"I'm so sorry, Noah. I didn't mean to barge in. My only concern was how hungry you and Lili would be." She held up her hands. "I promise I won't violate your privacy again. Unless I'm invited."

His eyebrow arched.

"Which I won't be, I'm sure. But I wanted you to know…"

A corner of his mouth lifted. "No problem. I wanted to thank you for the meal. It had been a long day. We were both exhausted. Lili had reached that hangry point of no return. There would have been a meltdown if your food hadn't been on the table when we got back." He cocked his head. "I'm not only referring to Lili. You saved the both of us."

She blinked. "You're not upset with me?"

"Absolutely not. The manicotti was delicious. Thank you."

Clutching the plates to her chest, she willed her heartbeat to settle. "I'm so glad." She smiled at him.

He smiled at her. Their gazes held.

"Anyway." He ran his hand over his head. "I wanted to..." His brows drew together. "To..."

"Return the plates?" She held up said plates.

He threw her a grateful smile. "Exactly. Before Lili and I left for the day."

They each took a quick glance through the open door. Felix sat on his haunches, licking his paws. Lili soared through the air on the swing.

"I hope you two are doing something fun this morning."

He leaned his shoulder against the wall. "I'm meeting the square beautification committee for a final inspection of the gazebo. And then I'm all yours."

Chloe's eyes widened.

"Not all yours. I mean," he sputtered, abruptly straightening. "I'll be working at the arts center." He pulled at the collar of his blue shirt.

A blue she couldn't help but notice brought out the vivid blue of his eyes.

"I promised Lili afterward we could pack a picnic and go for a hike. As a local, any beginner trail suggestions you could give me?"

"There's a trail not far from Truelove. What time is your meeting?"

"Not until ten o'clock, but I want to make sure the jobsite is spotless before they get there."

"What about Lili?"

"Lili understands I have to finish my work. She's good about entertaining herself." He frowned. "Perhaps too good."

Chloe brightened. "I have the best idea ever." She bounced a little.

He gave her a lopsided grin. "Why am I suddenly afraid?"

"What if Lili were to keep me company this morning?"

"That's kind of you to offer to take care of Lili but—"

"I'd love to hang out with her." She stilled. "Unless you think she'd be bored."

"Who could be bored hanging out with you?"

"That's sweet of you to say, but I can think of several who might disagree."

He made a face. "*Sweet* was not a word usually associated with somebody like Noah Knightley. Not good for my bad-boy image."

"I believe an image is all it ever was with you."

His eyes warmed. "You think so?"

"I do." She fingered the gold filigree necklace that lay against her throat. "I've seen you with Lili. I think Noah Brenden is a very decent guy."

"Thank you. That may be one of the nicest things anyone has ever said to me." He smiled. "I still don't believe anyone would find hanging out with you boring."

She gave him a world-weary look. "Trust me, they do."

"Like who?"

"My brothers."

He laughed. "Speaking from experience, brothers are hardly the best judge of their sister."

She tilted her head. "I didn't know you had a sister."

"I thought I—never mind." He shook his head. "She was my twin sister."

Chloe raised her eyebrows. "There are two of you in the world?"

"But yesterday, I explained..."

"What?"

He sighed. "She's no longer with us."

Chloe stiffened. "I'm sorry. I didn't mean to be insensitive. I didn't know."

"Not many people do. I like to keep my private life private."

Something he'd perfected to an art form.

"I don't talk to many people about her because it leads to awkward questions, but I'd like you to know. She was a special person."

"You were close."

He studied his work boots. "I've felt lost since she died. Like part of me went missing, too. The best part."

Pain lanced her heart. Sadness for the losses he'd suffered in his life.

"My brothers are annoying, but I can't imagine my life without them. I'm honored you felt comfortable sharing her with me."

"I'm sure you get that a lot, don't you?"

She blinked. "What?"

"People confiding in you."

"I have that kind of face." She slumped. "I'm sorry."

"Stop apologizing for being you. You have a generous, kind heart. No wonder people feel safe sharing their secrets with you."

He glanced at his cell phone. "I should get going." His mouth curved. "I lose track of time when I'm talking to you."

"I'm sor—"

He cut his eyes at her.

"I mean, I'm glad you find me interesting…" She flushed. "Not interesting-interesting. I mean…" What did she mean? "Not boring," she rasped.

He cocked his head. "I find you exceptionally easy to talk to, which is why I expect you're so good with your students. Of course, I also find you endlessly entertaining."

"Is that a good thing?"

He grinned. "A very good thing. You make me laugh."

She suspected he was a man who needed to laugh more.

"Glad to be of service. My brothers laugh at me all the time."

"I'm not laughing *at* you, Chloe. Just *with* you. Thanks for being my friend."

She also suspected he didn't have many of those—probably because he didn't allow many people to get close to him.

Had he erected those high, strong walls as a result of the craziness that followed stars like Noah Knightley? Or had his unusual childhood plus losing both his sister and Lili's mother taught him to keep others at a safe distance?

She didn't mind being his friend. Anything else would be out of the question. In fact, knowing where she stood with him took away some of the nervousness she felt in his presence.

He fingered his chin. "If you really don't mind, I know Lili would prefer to spend the morning with you."

"I don't mind." She smiled. "Is it okay if Lili goes with me to run a few errands around town?"

"Sure, but be warned. Everything takes twice as long with a four-year-old tagging along."

Chloe fluttered her hand. "Lili and I will have a blast. I'll bring her over to the square."

"Thank you." He turned to go. "I'll take Lili's hat and sunscreen with me so we can head to the trail after the meeting ends."

"We'll see you soon."

He went over to the swing to explain the new plan to Lili.

She looked forward to spending time with Lili. And she couldn't deny she also looked forward to seeing Noah later, too.

Chloe made a deliberate effort to tamp down her excitement. She and Noah were just friends. Story of her life—everybody's best buddy, little sis and gal pal. But if Noah only wanted friendship, she'd be the best friend he ever had.

In the meantime, she just needed to get the butterflies in her belly, wobbly knee thing under control.

Easier said than done.

Chapter Six

～

A few minutes later, Noah drove off toward town, and Lili ran over to Chloe. "What shall we do now, Miss Randolph?"

"Let's give Felix his medicine and make sure he has everything he needs."

The cat's bed and bowls had been relocated to the loft apartment yesterday.

Chloe tapped her finger on her chin. "Then how about we put together a picnic lunch for you and your da—your Noah?"

After taking care of Felix, they returned to the house, careful not to wake Travis.

Chloe put Lili in charge of spreading mayonnaise on slices of loaf bread.

She pulled sandwich meat out of the fridge. "Ham or turkey? What do you and Noah like?"

"Ham for Noah and turkey for me, please."

They were bagging chips and cookies when Travis ambled into the kitchen.

Her eyes darted to the clock on the wall. "I hope we didn't wake you."

Travis was dressed in an old T-shirt and cargo shorts. "I wanted to get an early start on my weekend off. I'm headed to Alan's. We're going fishing with Squirt."

She wrapped the sandwiches in wax paper. "Monday you're on days again?"

"Yep."

She tucked a few freezer packs into an insulated cooler. "Good."

"You worry too much, sis."

Lips pursed, she added the food to the cooler. "You don't worry enough."

"What's the chance of me getting one of those to go?"

Lili lifted the spatula. "I'll make you a sandwich, Travis."

Chloe took out extra slices of bread and laid them on the counter.

Lili slathered on mayo. "Who's Squirt, Travis?"

He leaned his elbows on the counter. "Alan is our older brother. I call Alan's son Squirt. He's about your age."

She handed Lili several slices of turkey to place atop the bread.

"The booster seat in Miss Randolph's car belongs to him?"

Chloe passed the little girl a slice of Colby jack cheese to layer on next. "That's right."

Her brother poured coffee from the carafe into a work thermos. "Have you ever been fishing, Lili?"

The child shook her head.

"Maybe one Saturday while you and your—"

"Noah." Chloe gave him a meaningful look.

"Maybe while you and your *Noah* are in Truelove, you two could come fishing with me. That way, you could meet the Squirt for yourself." He cut his eyes to his sister. "We'd love the chance to get to know you and your Noah better."

Chloe elbowed him.

He dodged out of her reach. "Just trying to be friendly."

"And nosy."

"Love you, too, sis."

"What you need is a good woman in your life, Sergeant." She tucked a handful of cookies into a sandwich bag for Alan and her nephew. "Maybe I should introduce you to our local veterinarian."

His eyes went wide. "Uh...no."

"You're not scared of Ingrid, are you?"

"Me and every man in a three-county area."

Ingrid could come off as extremely intimidating.

"Perhaps if you got to know her better…"

He held up his hands. "Thanks, but no thanks."

Smirking, she gave him his lunch. "If you're sure."

"You'll have to find some other blood sacrifice for that blond, blue-eyed ice queen." He backed toward the door. "See you gals later."

Lili waved. "Enjoy your sandwich."

His face softened. "Thank you, Lili." He wagged his finger at Chloe. "You could learn a thing or two from this sweet little girl, sis."

She raised a sponge to hurl at him.

"Okay. Okay. I'm going already." He ducked out the kitchen door.

Lili giggled. "Travis is so funny."

"He's something all right. Like I'd really wish my friend Ingrid on him. He should be so blessed."

"Noah met the better-narian. So he's blessed, right?"

Frowning, she gave the countertop an extra thorough scrub. Noah hadn't been into Ingrid, had he? Not that it was any of her business if he had. But he hadn't, right?

"Would you like to see my music room, sweetheart?"

Lili smiled. "Yes, please."

They went into the front room she used as her home office. Sitting on the piano bench, she helped Lili find middle C. She showed her how to place her right hand on the keyboard and play a simple scale.

At the sound of the tinkling keys, Lili laughed. "I love music."

"I love music, too."

"Noah used to have a piano, but now he only has his guitar." The child ran the fingers of her right hand up and down the scale like Chloe had taught her. "He sings with me at night before bed."

"That sounds nice."

"I love it when he sings with me. He showed me a picture of him and my mom playing the piano, but he says a piano won't fit in the truck." She giggled. "Noah is silly sometimes."

The more Chloe got to know Noah, the more she realized there were sides to him she hadn't known existed.

"Will you teach me to play a song on the piano, Miss Randolph?"

"How about one we sing at school? 'Twinkle, Twinkle Little Star' is a great song to begin with. It only has six notes."

It didn't take the little girl long to master the simple melody.

She glanced at her watch. "You practice while I run upstairs to get my purse. Then we'll head over to Main Street. Soon it'll be time for you and Noah to go on your adventure."

Upstairs, she took a moment to dab lip gloss on her lips and run a brush through her hair. Not because she was going to see Noah. She made a face at the mirror. But because she naturally liked to look her best. Right.

Coming downstairs, she was surprised to hear Lili picking out a tune on the piano that sounded like "Mary Had a Little Lamb." It consisted of only four notes, but it was also a much longer song with a trickier tempo. Somehow Lili had managed to duplicate it.

The child had an ear for music, no surprise considering who her father was. Perhaps while they were in Truelove, she could convince Noah to allow Lili to take piano lessons. Talent should be nurtured, in her opinion.

She swept into the music room. "You are so clever to have figured out the song by yourself."

Lili's eyes shone.

"Maybe you can play it for Noah later." She held out her

hand. "I need to take care of a few things downtown and drop off my car to get the tires rotated."

With Lili buckled into the car seat and the picnic cooler stowed in the trunk, she drove toward the town square. Rounding the corner, she spotted Noah at the gazebo with the mayor, GeorgeAnne Allen and Jeffrey.

Grimacing, she parked outside the pharmacy.

"What's wrong, Miss Randolph?"

She readjusted her expression. "Just going over the to-do list in my head." Including steering her suspicious eldest brother clear of Noah.

At the drugstore, they ran into IdaLee chatting with the young woman manning the cash register. The pretty brunette was a current prospect for several matchmaker projects in the works. Which reminded Chloe that she needed to check on Ingrid. The older ladies had long ago washed their hands of the prickly veterinarian. But once she found the perfect match for Ingrid, she'd prove herself worthy to join their exalted ranks as a full-fledged member of the Truelove Matchmakers.

Later on the sidewalk, Lili slipped her hand into Chloe's. The unconscious sweetness of the gesture made her eyes mist. They walked down the block to the Hair Raisers salon.

On a Saturday morning, her best friend, Mollie Atkinson, had a full house of customers. A slightly chemical aroma hung in the air. Lili wrinkled her nose. Perusing magazines, several ladies underneath hooded dryers waved at Chloe.

Behind a salon chair, Mollie used the pointy end of a comb to part a portion of Mrs. Desmond's hair and wind it around a small curler. Seated on the black-and-white tiled floor, Mrs. Desmond's tiny Chihuahua barked a greeting.

Mollie smiled at the little girl. "Hello, Lili. Chloe has told me so much about you I feel like I know you already." She helped the older lady over to a dryer and set the timer. "I can go over the guest list now."

Lili enjoyed "driving" the red kid car on a nearby salon chair while she and Mollie finalized plans for getting friends together for a cookout. No one in the salon even pretended not to eavesdrop. Such was small-town life. Like the Mason Jar, Hair Raisers was a hub on the Truelove grapevine.

Chloe consulted a list on her phone. "The Gibsons are coming."

Mollie scrolled through her cell. "Ditto for Clay and Kelsey."

"Great." The McKendrys were fun. "Just need a few more single guys to balance out our single lady contingent."

Thanks to the matchmakers, their ranks were steadily diminishing, but there were still a few eligible men in Truelove, and Chloe intended to use the opportunity to jumpstart her efforts on Ingrid's behalf.

Mollie fluttered her lashes. "Hunky Lieutenant Bradley at the firehouse RSVPed."

She rolled her eyes. "As a married woman, you have no business noticing he's hunky."

Mollie sniffed. "I'm married, not blind. Speaking of hunky, you invited your brothers, didn't you?"

"If I must," she growled.

The hairstylist glanced at Lili. "What about your carpenter?"

She bristled. "He's not *my* anything."

"But he's single, isn't he?" Mollie dropped her voice. "Is he widowed?"

"I don't know the details, but he is a single parent, yes." She lowered her voice, too. "What about Lili, though?"

"There'll be lots of kids there, including my Oliver. It's a family cookout." Mollie arched her eyebrow. "You should definitely invite Lili's dad. 'Cause if the lieutenant is hunky, the carpenter is definitely in a category all by himself." Mollie made a show of fanning her face. "Ooh la la."

Chloe blushed.

"Don't you think so?"

What she thought about Noah didn't matter.

"He won't come." She pressed her lips together. "He doesn't get out much."

"All the more reason to invite him. The Brendens would probably appreciate getting to know more people in True-love." Mollie's eyes narrowed. "Why don't you want to include him? What's wrong with him?"

Chloe crossed her arms. "Nothing is wrong with him."

"Or maybe you want to keep him to yourself?"

She glowered at her best friend. "That's not it." Absolutely not the reason. Was it?

"Then you'll invite him?"

Unable to summon another excuse, she nodded.

"Fantastic. Can't wait to meet him." A dryer dinged. "Gotta go." Mollie walked away. "Talk to you later."

With the certain knowledge Noah would turn down the invitation, Chloe and Lili retraced their steps to her car. But every few feet, they were stopped by townspeople eager to meet the cute little girl and catch up with Chloe's family news.

Unused to such attention, Lili hugged her side, but gradually her shyness faded away, especially with young moms like Callie McAbee, who had five-year-old Micah with her.

When Callie laid her hand on her softly swelling abdomen, she realized her friend must be expecting again. Callie's third. She congratulated her.

Older folks asked about when Chloe's parents were due to fly home from Florida.

"After Memorial Day. Just in time for the music festival."

It was one of the things she loved most about her hometown—the feeling of belonging to a caring community.

Myra Penry, town CPA and her mother's friend, patted her arm. "I know how proud Ann and Dennis are of your efforts on behalf of our dear town."

"It's been a labor of love."

Chloe's gaze wandered toward the gazebo only to catch Noah's eye. Her heart accelerated. Mollie wasn't wrong. In a category all his own, handsome didn't begin to describe Lili's heartthrob dad.

Face flushing, she tore her gaze to Myra's ten-year-old granddaughter, Emma Cate Gibson, who was chatting a mile a minute with Lili. The four-year-old didn't contribute much to the conversation, but the smile on her face revealed how much she enjoyed being with other children.

Noah had chosen a lonely path for not only himself but Lili, too. Perhaps he didn't feel the loneliness. Not everyone was a people person like her.

She and Lili drove around the block to Zach's automotive repair shop.

Perhaps Noah had loved Lili's mother so much that after her death there was no place in his heart for anyone else.

Would she ever know what it would be like to be loved like that? Her gaze flitted toward the square.

Maybe someday.

Noah spotted Chloe's car outside the pharmacy. He followed their progress into the hair salon. They were inside for a long time, which was good since he could then give his full attention to the committee members. The bank VP in particular had a lot of questions about everything.

In his early thirties, with slicked back hair and expensive Italian loafers—which Noah recognized 'cause he used to own a pair back in the day—the banker didn't fit Truelove's usual laidback mountain vibe.

Noah also got the sense the banker was looking to find fault with his craftsmanship. Confident in his work, Noah answered all his questions. The gazebo had been a joy to restore. He was proud of the finished product, which the citizens of Truelove could enjoy for another century.

His attention drifted as Chloe and Lili emerged from the hair salon. Based on the number of people who stopped to talk with her, Chloe seemed to be everyone's favorite person. He was also aware of how everyone made much of his little girl.

At first, she clung to Chloe. But Lili slowly unfurled. Chloe Randolph was good for his niece. Under her maternal, nurturing presence, Lili blossomed.

He kept an eye on them as Chloe parked outside the automotive repair shop. A wiry, ordinary looking guy ambled out of the garage bay. Picking up Chloe, he swung her around.

Noah's mouth fell open.

Laughing, Chloe patted the mechanic's shoulder, and he set her on her feet again. Old friends. Noah's gut did a slow burn. More than friends?

GeorgeAnne Allen cleared her throat. "Are we boring you, Mr. Brenden?"

His gaze swung to the handful of committee members staring at him with mixed expressions of amusement. However, the banker scowled at him. If Noah hadn't known for a fact they had never met before, he would have sworn the suit had it in for him.

"Sorry. You were saying, Miss GeorgeAnne?"

Her eyebrow arched. "I was saying that with the completion of the gazebo, so goes the last painful reminder of the day the tornado swept through our beloved town."

Mayor Watson—who doubled as Santa on the Square during the holidays—clapped him on the back. "We can move forward toward the final project to revitalize Truelove—the restoration of the Lyric." He chuckled. "I hear your considerable skills will also be applied to that. Truelove will forever be in your debt."

The banker's lip curled. "Hardly."

He had no idea what the man's problem was with him, but he and the dude were obviously never going to be bosom buddies.

The man folded his arms across his three-piece suit. "Brenden's 'so-called talents' have not come cheap. The beautification fund will be completely drained."

Speaking of which, somebody was supposed to hand over a check to him this morning for his work on the gazebo.

GeorgeAnne's lips thinned. "Stop acting as if the funds came out of your pocket and pay the man, Jeffrey."

Noah's eyes narrowed. Why did that name ring a bell?

Holding Lili's hand, Chloe crossed the street to the square, snagging his attention once again.

"Well, well." GeorgeAnne Allen thumped his back, jerking him from his reverie. A look of eminent satisfaction crossed her wrinkled face. "That's worked itself out then."

He scratched his head. "Ma'am?"

GeorgeAnne turned to go with the other departing committee members. "You and your little family are a much welcome addition to our community."

"A temporary addition to Truelove," he called after her. "But thank you."

"You may have the Double Name Club's endorsement, but I don't trust you," the banker snarled. "The sooner you leave Truelove, the better."

The stuffed shirt could use taking down a peg or two, but Noah wasn't looking for trouble.

"You'll get no argument from me." Reining in his temper, he held out his hand. "But first, my money."

With a show of reluctance, the banker handed over the check. As Noah reached for it, the suit kept a stubborn hold on the paper. "Just so we understand each other, Brenden."

What was his deal?

"No worries." Noah bared his teeth. "Can't wait to shake the dust from this town." He yanked the check from the banker's grasp.

The man grunted. "While you're in my town, you better watch your step."

He'd had about enough of this chump. "Oh, yeah?" Jeffrey balled his fist.

Chloe inserted herself between them. "What's going on?" She pushed them apart.

He and the suit fell back a step.

"What're you doing here, Jeffrey?" she hissed. "You're not on the beautification committee."

He adjusted his tie. "I volunteered to do the honors in place of the town manager."

It was at that moment Noah spotted the resemblance. The banker possessed the same dark hair and eyes as his siblings. "This suit is your brother?"

"Yes, he is," she sighed.

Jeffrey smoothed a well-manicured hand over his hair. "Just trying to do my civic duty."

"More like trying to cause trouble," she muttered.

"Hey, Miss Randolph's brother." The little girl tugged at his coat. "My name's Lili Brenden."

Brother or no brother, if Jeffrey hurt Lili's feelings, he'd make sure he regretted it.

Eyes wide, Jeffrey looked at Lili as if he'd never seen a child before. "Uh... Hey?"

"I saw your picture at Miss Randolph's house." She tilted her head. "My teacher says you work at a bank and count money."

He glared at his sister. "Among other things."

"I'm good at counting. I can count all the way to forty. You want me to show you?"

"Uh..." Jeffrey's gaze darted. "Okay. I guess."

"One...two...three..."

"What have you unleashed, Chloe Randolph?" Tucking his hands in his arms, Noah rocked on his heels. "One morning with you and Lili has become a social butterfly."

She batted her lashes at him. "You're welcome."

"...seventeen...eighteen..." Lili's smile faltered. "Oh, no." She clapped her hand over her mouth.

"Nineteen?" Jeffrey gently suggested. "Nines can be hard."

Lili's head bobbed, setting the braids a quiver. "Nineteen... twenty..." She caught hold of Jeffrey's hand. A smile flickered across his rather austere features.

"Kudos to Lili," Chloe whispered. "For charming the savage beast, otherwise known as my eldest brother."

Noah pointed to the blue bag hanging from Chloe's shoulder. "What's that?"

"Lili and I made lunch for your hike. She told me what you liked." She smiled and his heart ratcheted.

What he liked was Chloe Randolph. More than was good for either one of them.

He swallowed. Hard. "I was going to swing by the café before we headed out."

"Now you don't have to."

A trace of honeysuckle wafted in his direction. His mind turned to mush. It was hard to keep his wits about him when he was with her.

"...thirty-eight...thirty-nine..." At some point, Jeffrey had joined Lili in the count up. "Forty!"

In mutual triumph, the banker and the little girl grinned at each other. Then, as if afraid his face might freeze into a smile, Jeffrey's expression became stern once more.

Loosening his hand from Lili's, he gave her a small pat on her head. "Thanks for that."

She beamed at Chloe's brother. "You're welcome. Next time, let's try for a hundred, okay?"

His brown eyes flicked to Chloe. "Sure?"

"Something to look forward to, Jeffrey." She motioned. "Don't let us keep you from the rest of your weekend."

He scowled at Noah. "I trust you'll remember our little chat, Brenden."

Noah tapped his finger to his forehead. "Like it was branded in my memory bank, Randolph."

Her brother stalked away. That guy was trouble. The sooner Noah departed Truelove, the better for everyone. Himself, most of all.

Chloe frowned. "What did he say to you?"

"Nothing worth repeating."

Lili flung herself at him. "Can we go hiking now?"

Noah gathered the child in his arms. "You're not supposed to talk to strangers, Lil."

"Mr. Jeffrey's not a stranger. He's Miss Randolph's brother."

A conclusion which his niece had arrived at far sooner than Noah.

Chloe squatted beside Lili. "It was very nice of you to talk to Jeffrey."

"I liked him." Lili leaned into Noah. "He seemed sad, but I think I cheered him up with our counting."

Chloe blinked. "He seemed sad to you?"

Lili nodded. "I decided to do what you do, Miss Randolph. Make him feel better."

Chloe looked at Noah. "Is that what I do?"

He nodded. "The Chloe Effect."

"The what?"

"You must have been really hungry when you made lunch, Lili-bell." He hefted the bag. "Seems like a lot of food here."

She giggled. "Where are we going, Noah?"

He looked at Chloe. "Suggestions?"

"I can point you in the direction of the closest ranger station." She got to her feet. "But first, I feel I should apologize for my brother."

Suddenly, he was in no hurry to walk away. Perhaps because he didn't like being told what to do. Or maybe because of reasons he wasn't ready to admit to himself, Noah wasn't eager for his time with Chloe to end.

"You have nothing to apologize for." He pursed his lips. "What would you say to coming hiking with us?"

She gaped at him. "You want me to go with you and Lili?"

Hands clasped under her chin, Lili bounced up and down. "Oh, please say you'll come. Please, Miss Randolph."

"You know the best trails. And thanks to you, there's plenty of food. I'm willing to share if you are."

In Colorado, Chloe had proven immune to the old Knightley charm. But just to test the waters, Noah threw her his trademark crooked grin.

She twisted the earring on her earlobe. "I wouldn't want to intrude." Her gaze dropped to the ground.

Just as he'd suspected. He sighed. Totally immune.

He kicked at the grass with his boot. "You wouldn't be intruding."

"Please, please, Miss Randolph..."

"If you think it would mean a lot to Lili."

"Not only Lili."

Her head snapped up.

They looked at each other a long moment. Somewhere underneath a rhododendron, a robin trilled.

Chloe blushed a becoming shade of pink. "I-I'd love to join you."

Something took flight in his heart.

Chloe smiled. "Let the adventure begin."

Indeed.

Chapter Seven

Clouds drifted lazily across a brilliant blue sky. Noah glanced at the petite music therapist hiking the forested trail beside him. The tangy scent of evergreens hung in the air.

Surging ahead, Lili emerged into a clearing dotted with spring wildflowers. Her arms extended, she twirled around. "What about here, Noah?"

"A perfect spot." Chloe motioned toward the valley. "A clear view of Truelove."

He laid the blanket over a level spot in the tall grass. Chloe distributed the contents of the bag. Lili only took a few bites of her sandwich before she was running around the meadow again.

"Stay where I can see you," Noah called.

His eyes flicked to Chloe. "There's been a huge difference in her self-confidence since you started working with her."

"Music allows her to express herself." Chloe wrapped her arms around her updrawn knees. "A Brenden family legacy?"

He toyed with a blade of grass. "I hope it's her only Brenden family legacy."

"Is your mother still in your life?"

"At age sixteen, my mother ran away from home to join a rock band. She was a train wreck. When we were nine, she did me and my sister the tremendous favor of dropping us at my grandparents. We never saw her again. She overdosed two months later."

"I'm so sorry."

He let his shoulders rise and fall.

"You inherited your talent from her?"

"And possibly from dear ole Dad. We never knew which guy on the bus was our father. Probably better that way." He sighed. "I want so much better for Lili than the chaotic childhood I had, but how much better is a pickup truck?"

"Noah! Miss Randolph! Look!"

Lili pointed at a yellow-and-black swallowtail. Flitting about the clearing, she chased after the butterfly.

"Yet your music became a great solace to you."

Stretching full length, he propped one elbow on the blanket. "Music was everything. A way out from a dead-end small town in the middle of Nowheresville. After my grandparents passed, there was no reason to stay. There were no jobs."

"Truelove has been intentional about investing in our town."

He lay back on the blanket. "What led you to get involved?"

"I got tired of watching friends being forced to leave town for opportunity and never come back."

"So you decided to stay."

"I decided to utilize my skills and invest in its people."

He sat up. "Truelove seems to be thriving."

"We've operated on a philosophy of 'use the assets you have.'" Her face softened. "Truelove has so many things going for it. Between the mountains and the river, it's a fantastic place."

Below, the river glinted like a silver ribbon around the small town.

"There's also a rich cultural tradition in the Appalachians of storytelling, handicrafts and music." Sitting forward, she ticked them off on her fingers. "But our biggest asset is our people. We've encouraged neighbors to help neighbors. A rising tide lifts all boats. If everybody does one small thing like paint their front door or plant flowers in their front yard—"

"Or restore an iconic gazebo on the town square."

She smiled. "We believe small acts of hope lead to big results."

"Faith becomes sight."

She nudged him with her shoulder. "Look at you catching the vision."

"Almost makes me want to live here."

Her mouth quirked. "Give the town a month to work its magic, and you'll become a diehard Truelove fan for life."

She told him about the impromptu piano lesson that morning. "Would you allow me to give Lili private lessons once a week? At no cost to you, of course."

"I'm not a pauper, Chloe."

Her eyes widened. "Of course, you're not. If you could've seen her joy at the piano… The music was such a gift to her."

Noah rubbed the back of his neck. "I'm not sure encouraging Lili in that direction would be a good thing."

She tilted her head. "It proved transformative for you."

"Or did the music just perpetuate my family's dysfunction?"

"Aren't you viewing the gift through the lens of your mother's tragedy instead of how it made you feel?"

He shook his head. "With your perfect family, it's hard for you to understand why I'm wary of traveling that path again."

"My family is far from perfect."

He held up his hands. "That wasn't meant as a criticism. Yours is the type of family I always wanted."

"People here have their sorrows same as the rest of the world. The difference is we know where to turn when life gets hard."

"To God, you mean?"

She told him about the Dolan family, who owned a local equestrian center and suffered the loss of their toddler a few years ago.

He winced. "I would die if anything happened to Lili."

"At first, Jack and Kate blamed each other." Her eyes watered. "But their renewed love for each other has been an inspiration for me to see how God can bring beauty out of brokenness."

"Lili has been God's precious gift to me."

Chloe touched his sleeve. "God never meant for us to walk through life alone. If you'd be interested in attending our little church while you and Lili are here, you'd be most welcome."

"Perhaps if I'd grown up with that kind of community around me, I might have made better choices."

"There's a children's church for kids Lili's age."

He nodded. "That sounds great."

As a cloud passed over the meadow, her smile dimmed. "I get so aggravated with Jeffrey, I forget to show my own brother the compassion God wants us to show others."

"He's different from you and Travis."

"Like you, growing up, Jeffrey couldn't wait to get out of Truelove."

He wasn't sure he liked being compared to her uptight brother.

"Jeff was on a fast track in a lucrative corporate career until his wife cheated on him with his so-called best friend. Behind the bitterness, he doesn't think we see how heartbroken he feels. Jeffrey had to start his life over in Truelove."

Noah did his periodic sweep of the meadow, tracking Lili's whereabouts. The little girl squatted not six feet away, next to a clump of wildflowers.

"Hope you don't suffer from seasonal allergies. The bouquet she's putting together is probably for you."

Chloe laughed. "It'll be the nicest bouquet anyone has ever given me."

"I can't believe that's true." Then, because he couldn't help himself, he fished for information he had no business caring about. "A pretty girl like you I'm sure has loads of admirers."

"Thank you for the compliment, but most men never get past my brothers, although there was a guy in college..."

His gut lurched. "What happened?"

"The long-distance relationship didn't survive the summer I spent in Colorado." Her gaze flickered. "Where I met you."

His chest tightened. She almost made it sound like... No. Impossible. She hadn't given him the time of day that summer. "No one else since then?" He couldn't resist probing.

She gave him a funny look. "Only my brother Alan has found true love. The rest of us are too busy with our careers. I know you think I could talk to a signpost—"

"Because it's true?"

She swatted his arm, but smiled. "However, I don't usually go around telling this stuff about my family, but I like talking to you."

He liked talking to her, too. Noah felt ridiculously pleased at her trust in him. It would be way too easy to fall in love with someone like Chloe Randolph.

When Lili returned, thrusting the yellow ragweed wildflower bouquet at Chloe, she expressed complete delight.

Grabbing his hand, Lili tugged at him. "Let's play a game."

He allowed himself to be pulled upright.

Chloe rose. "What game do you want to play, sweetie pie?"

"Let's play tag."

He folded his arms. "She wants to be It. She likes the counting part." He winked. "And being bossy."

Chloe ignored him. "Should I run now, Lili?"

Lili shook her head. "First, let me 'plain the rules to you."

Bossy, he mouthed.

"This is serious, Noah." Lili pursed her small lips. "Rules are important. You need to pay attention."

Chloe elbowed him. "Yeah, Noah. You need to listen."

"Number one," Lili adopted a schoolteacher-ish tone. "I'll close my eyes and count to fifty while you hide."

He whistled. "Up to fifty is it now?"

Chloe's mouth quirked. "What's the next rule?"

"You have to stay in the meadow." She wagged her finger at them. "No cheating by hiding in the woods."

Chloe grinned. "What about home base?"

Lili pointed to a large elm in the middle of the meadow. "The tree is safe, but you can only stay there for ten seconds."

His eyebrows rose. "How fair is that?"

"I'm a little girl, Noah." She propped her hand on her hip. "I can't run as fast or as far as you."

Chloe laughed.

"Okay!" Lili clapped her hands. "You better run and hide before I find you." She squeezed her eyelids shut. "One… two…"

Chloe blinked. "We're playing now?"

"…five…"

He grinned. "We better get going in case she has trouble with the nines again and we lose our fifty-second head start."

Because it seemed the most natural thing in the world, he grabbed her hand. They ran toward the tree.

"Shouldn't we go in opposite directions?" she panted.

"Don't want to make it too hard for her." He rolled his eyes. "Her being a little girl and all."

Reaching the tree, he peered into the branches. "Limbs look sturdy enough."

"Enough for what?"

"To climb."

Her mouth dropped. "You want us to climb this tree? Isn't that cheating?"

Noah did a visual sweep of the meadow. "Not many choices for hiding if we keep out of the woods. We'll take a breather and let her run around the meadow a few times before we let her catch us."

Chloe eyed the tree canopy. "I'm not sure about this."

"Do you only climb trees when a cat's life is at stake?"

"Look how well that turned out for me."

"Didn't turn out so bad from where I was standing."

"If I fall out of this tree, Noah Brenden—"

"You won't fall, but if you do, I'll catch you, I promise."

She pointed. "The branches are higher than the one in the square."

"Just put your foot in my hands." He went down on his knee and laced his fingers together. "I'll give you a boost."

"Fifty!" Lili yelled. "Ready or not, here I come."

She placed her foot in his hands. He heaved her toward the branch. Grabbing hold, she climbed to a higher spot.

"Come out, come out wherever you are," Lili shouted.

He pulled himself up to a large branch on the opposite side of the trunk.

From their perch, they watched Lili race around the perimeter of the field.

"I almost forgot. Colton's wife, Mollie, wanted me to invite you and Lili to a cookout at her house next Saturday."

"A cookout?"

"Nothing fancy. A bring-your-own-lawn-chair kind of thing. Some of Lili's playmates at school will be there. I thought you might like to meet their parents and get to know other people in town besides me." She blushed. "Although, I'm sure you know lots more people in Truelove than just me."

She was doing that nervous talkative thing again.

"No worries if you can't come. You probably have plans."

"I don't."

She went on as if he hadn't spoken. "I totally understand if you have a ton of other stuff you'd rather do on a weekend."

"Can't think of a thing. Sounds fun. Count me in. What can I bring?"

"Why would you want to come?" She gaped at him. "You don't like people."

"Don't want to get too predictable. Besides, certain people have a way of growing on me."

Her cheeks went pink, filling him with a secret pleasure.

"Noah! Miss Randolph! Where are you?"

He grinned. "Hope you're ready to run."

"I'm ready."

A breeze ruffled a tendril of her hair, billowing it across her cheek. His breath hitched. "I'm ready, too. Let me climb down first, and I'll help you."

Noah clambered down, ready to guide her foot placement. But she didn't need his help. She slid into the circle of his arms. "You have the most stellar tree-climbing skills of anyone I've ever met."

"Hardly." Smiling, she leaned against the rough bark of the trunk. "There's plenty better than me."

"I'm beginning to doubt there's anyone better than you, Chloe."

Their gazes locked. Pinpricks of mutual attraction danced down his spine. "Would it be okay if I kissed you?" He gulped. "I've been wanting to since the day you fell out of the tree into my arms."

In truth, his longing to kiss her stretched further back than merely a week ago. To an almost forgotten day when their paths crossed for the first time in an open-air amphitheater for a preproduction rehearsal.

Carrying his guitar, he'd walked across the stage to the microphone for a sound check. He'd turned to cue the pianist. Chloe had been at the keyboard. Their eyes met. Something in her gaze had stirred something inside him. A recognition. An acknowledgement.

Like now.

Did she want him to kiss her? Had he imagined the moment between them in Colorado? Why was he even thinking about—

"Yes," she whispered. A vein in the hollow of her throat pulsed.

The buzzing in his brain quieted.

Unlike that summer when he'd put aside the pull he'd felt for the intern for the sake of his ambition, there was no longer a need to hesitate.

He swept his thumb across the apple of her cheek. His gaze dropped to her mouth. Her lips parted. His heart slammed against his ribcage. He gave her the opportunity to pull away if she wished. Yet she didn't. Her eyes closed.

This was a bad, bad idea. In a few weeks, he'd leave Truelove, never to return. This kiss could destroy the fragile terms of their still-new friendship.

But he touched his lips featherlight across her mouth anyway. Her arms went around his neck. She kissed him back.

For a second, he allowed himself to enjoy the sweetness of the moment. But reality intruded. None of his relationships ever worked.

Why should he think this one would now? And of all people, Chloe? A girl he had admired. A woman he liked far too much. If—when—any relationship with Lili's teacher went sour, as it inevitably would, it would be Lili who would suffer the most.

He pulled his mouth from hers. Her eyes flew open.

A small frown marred the smooth space between her perfect brows. "Is everything—"

"Noah!" Lili's tone had become impatient. "Miss Randolph! Where are you?"

Dropping his arms, he dashed out from under the tree canopy and straight into Lili's path.

"Tag!" The little girl crowed. "I got you, Noah."

Chloe ran out and allowed the little girl to tag her, too. "I probably should think about heading back to town." She gave him a probing look.

"But we just got here," Lili moaned. "We were having fun."

Chloe planted a quick kiss on her head. "We were having fun." She glanced at him. "Maybe we can come again soon."

Avoiding eye contact, he took Lili's hand. "Let's pack up the picnic."

Hiking the trail back to the truck, he felt Chloe's eyes upon him. The shy, swift smiles she threw his way. And her confusion when he didn't respond.

Driving down the mountain toward town, the pressure in his chest increased. Lili kept up a bright chatter with Chloe. But he could feel her sidelong looks.

On the outskirts of town, the truck passed the welcome sign. Truelove: Where True Love Awaits. Not something that applied to his situation.

"Is everything okay, Noah?" she asked when Lili finally paused for a breath.

The truck rattled over the bridge.

He throttled the wheel. "Do you want me to take you home, or drop you off at the repair shop?"

"If you'd take me to Zach, that would be great."

Veering around the square, he pulled into the parking lot at the auto repair shop. Chloe released her seat belt and reached in the back for the insulated bag.

She patted Lili's knee. "See you at home, sweetie pie." She slipped out of the truck. "It was such a lovely day. Thank you for inviting me."

It had been a lovely day. Until he'd ruined everything by kissing her. He shouldn't have done that. It was clear he'd given her the wrong idea. About his feelings, his intentions. About them as a couple.

Because of Lili—because of his past—there could never be a *them*.

Noah scrubbed his hand over his face. "Don't let us keep you."

Her smile faltered a sec, but Chloe Randolph was nothing if not a positive thinker. "I'll see you soon." She chuckled. "Since you live in my backyard."

Until he finished the work at the arts center, living in her backyard was going to be tricky. Lili was very attached to the music therapist. Not running into Chloe would be difficult.

The mechanic guy—Zach—came out of the open garage bay. "Chlo?"

She shut the door. Noah threw the truck into Reverse.

Lili waved. "Bye, Miss Randolph."

He backed onto the street. Chloe stared after them. He changed gears.

The last thing he saw before pulling away was the mechanic dude giving her a hug. And Chloe hugging him back.

Anger churned in his belly. At himself. At the situation. But mostly, for wanting something—wanting someone—he shouldn't.

He consoled himself with the knowledge that because he cared about her, he was doing her a favor. Later, it did not escape his notice that she didn't return to the house until after dark.

She'd probably spent the evening with Zach. Which bothered him. Far more than it should have.

He needed to set the record straight between them. Let her down gently. Cut her loose. He and Chloe were never going to happen.

Or so he told himself over and over that night as he lay awake into the wee hours of the morning, wrestling over what had happened. Trying to untangle the strange sense of rightness he felt when he was with her.

More than anything, that was what scared him. What made him want to pack up his truck and get out of Truelove tonight. Chloe was the marrying kind of girl. Because of his childhood, because of who he'd been—Noah was not.

Staring at the darkened ceiling, it didn't take much imagination to envision her future. A happy life that did not include him. A life far out of his reach.

He had a job to do at the Lyric. He would do it and leave. It was one kiss. Didn't mean anything. Could never mean anything with Chloe.

No more kissing. No more hanging out. No more anything.

Relieved to have settled the issue in his mind, he finally drifted off to sleep.

Groggy-eyed, he woke early the next morning with plenty of time to get Lili ready for church. He'd been sincere in wanting to help Lili to build a relationship with her heavenly Father.

There was also a longing within him to connect with a faith community. At least for the duration of their sojourn in Truelove.

Rubbing her eyes, Lili ventured out of her bedroom in search of breakfast. She climbed into her usual chair.

"Want to go to church this morning, Lili-bell?"

She tilted her head. "What do you do at church?"

Guilt smote him. *Forgive me, God.* She ought to know for herself what church was like.

He poured her a glass of milk. "There are stories about Jesus. There are prayers."

"Like we do every night at bedtime?"

"Exactly."

She nodded. "What else?"

"People sing."

Her face lit up. "I love singing. Let's go." She scrambled out of the chair.

A real Brenden, this niece of his.

She insisted on wearing one of her special outfits. A soft, butter-yellow dress he'd bought on impulse the last time they shopped. She also wanted her hair styled into a single braid like Chloe sometimes wore.

After viewing his dismal first attempt in the mirror, though, she got mad. "That doesn't look like Miss Randolph's hair."

"Maybe Miss Randolph ought to be the one fixing your hair then," he muttered.

A silent tear rolled down her cheek.

God, give me strength. Little-girl hair was going to be the death of him. He found a how-to video on his phone. Fifteen minutes and a lot of anguish later—mostly his—he secured the yellow silk bow into the end of the French braid.

Staring at herself in the mirror, a small smile curved the corners of her lips.

Thank You, God. If this morning's drama was any indication of what the teen years would be like, Noah was never going to make it.

She hugged his waist. "Do I look pretty?"

"Beautiful. Gorgeous. Absolutely stunning."

She giggled.

Actually, with her hair pulled back like that, he caught a brief, bittersweet glimmer of Lili's mother, his beloved sister.

"I love you, Noah."

"I love you, too, Lili-bell," he rasped.

Driving out of town, his stomach was in knots. He'd performed for thousands of people. No need to be nervous about a small country church. But his restlessness wasn't so much about church as it was about seeing Chloe.

The more he told himself to stop thinking about her, the more it left him wanting to kiss her again.

Nestled in a glade on the edge of town, the steeple brushed a picture-perfect Blue Ridge sky. He steered into the gravel parking lot. Lili waved at a little girl she recognized from her preschool class.

Her hand in his, they walked from the parking lot toward the church over the tiny footbridge spanning a small creek. Rushing water burbled over the moss-covered stones.

People stood around outside on the steps. He felt Lili shrink a little. Or maybe that was him. Above the soft murmur of voices were sweet sounds of birdsong. The apple-green leaves of a willow rustled in a light breeze.

He was contemplating making an unobtrusive withdrawal when Travis's hunter green truck steered into the parking lot. Seated in the passenger seat, Chloe spotted him and Lili. She lifted her hand. His heart thudding, he looked away.

Exit strategy thwarted, he found himself engulfed by the Double Name Club. ErmaJean and CoraFaye Dolan herded him toward children's church.

"Hey, Parker!" Lili called to ErmaJean's great-grandson.

Without a backward glance, she abandoned Noah at the door of her classroom. CoraFaye shooed him into the hall.

Suddenly, he recalled what Chloe had shared with him about the Dolans. He was still working out the nuances of who was related to who in Truelove, but he had a feeling the whippet-lean older woman had to be connected with Jack and Kate Dolan's tragic loss.

It was disconcerting the rush of empathy he felt for a woman who, until this moment, he'd regarded as a stranger. Caring was how small towns got their hooks into people. Good thing he was only passing through. Lili was the only one who he had room in his heart for.

He cleared his throat. "Maybe I should stay to make sure she's okay."

Parker shared his crayons with Lili. She smiled at her school friend.

CoraFaye raised her eyebrow. "Lili will be fine."

But would he?

She shut the door in his face. With no other options, he made his way to the sanctuary to face the mess he'd made of things with Chloe. Time to let her know in no uncertain terms where they stood with each other.

Nowhere.

Chapter Eight

On Sunday morning, she rode to church with Travis. Spotting Noah outside the sanctuary, she started to wave, but he must not have seen her before the Double Name Club swept him into the educational building. She'd see him soon enough.

She made a beeline for the main sanctuary. Feeling strangely protective of him, she didn't want him to have to face strangers alone. Yesterday in the meadow had been like a dream. His sweet, gentle kiss had her questioning everything she always believed she wanted from life.

That kiss had kept her awake into the wee hours of night. It had been too brief, but full of so many bright possibilities.

Her heart ached for him. He'd lost everyone he'd ever loved—his grandparents, his sister, Lili's mom. Abandoned by the one person who should have been there for him—his mother. No wonder he was wary of relationships.

It was important today be a success. Coming to church was no small step for him.

Squaring her shoulders, she prepared to ease his entry into Truelove society, but she was waylaid by Miss IdaLee inquiring about her parents.

On a mission to rescue Noah, she was unusually brief with the oldest matchmaker. Other friends tried to chat her up, but she dodged well-meaning attempts to shoot the breeze in an effort to locate the antisocial carpenter.

Travis and his pals blocked the steps into the foyer.

She pushed her brother's solid bulk aside. "Pardon me." She

edged around Fire Chief Will MacKenzie. "Coming through." She inched past Bridger Hollingsworth, Truelove's chief of police.

Inside the sanctuary, she found Noah warming a pew nearest the exit. She would have gone over to sit with him, but he turned his back on her.

She stopped so abruptly in the aisle, Travis bumped into her.

His shoulders hunched, Noah wouldn't meet her gaze. The emotional about-face was a surprise and not a good one. Her heart thudded in her chest. Was he snubbing her?

He'd been so quiet on the way back to town yesterday afternoon after their picnic, but she'd made excuses for him. Rationalized his brusqueness with her. Saw only what she wanted to see—a bad habit her brothers had often pointed out to her.

But obviously, Noah was feeling regret about their kiss. How delusional was she to imagine Noah Knightley would ever be seriously interested in her?

Heat enflamed her cheeks.

"Chlo?" Travis whispered in her ear. "Where do you want to sit?"

Pulling herself together, she turned away from the object of her misery and gestured toward the opposite side of the aisle. "Our usual spot."

She was proud how even her voice sounded. She lifted her chin and moved forward. Wondering how many people had witnessed Noah blow her off, she sank into the family pew. Travis eased down beside her.

"Oh. I'm sorry." She put her hand on his arm. "Maybe you want to sit with your friends?" With his schedule, her brother didn't get to attend church as often as he would like.

Travis nudged her shoulder with his. "I think I'll sit with you today."

Her heart warmed. "You don't have to babysit me. I'm fine. Truly."

"I know you're fine. Just feeling like we don't spend as much time together as we used to."

"Travis, we live in the same house."

He waved over Zach, who'd just ambled into the sanctuary.

Smiling, the garage owner moved toward them. "Got room for me?"

Chloe patted the seat beside her. "Always." At least someone was glad to see her.

Travis winked. "Perhaps we should think about getting the band back together. I know Alan would be in."

She laughed. "Let's imagine for a sec what Jeffrey would say about that?"

Travis grinned. "But it would be worth it to wind him up, wouldn't it?"

Her brother was the best. He knew how to coax her out of a mood. When Travis and Zach launched into a convoluted discussion regarding the finer points of car detailing, she zoned out.

For dignity's sake, she dared not turn her head in Noah's direction to see how he was faring all by himself. Probably just fine. He didn't like people. He liked being alone.

But this was Truelove.

People here were friendly—or incurably nosy, depending on one's point of view. It was like she had specially tuned radar when it came to him. Though she kept her face averted, she was painfully aware of him on the other side of the aisle. And, every time a sociable soul stopped to greet him.

Bless their sweet, well-meaning hearts. She pursed her lips. They'd soon learn the hard way like she had. *You can't help someone who doesn't want to be helped.*

She took a perverse satisfaction in imagining him squirming at Truelove's relentless pleasantness.

The service began. Reverend Bryant spoke on a passage about doing good to those who despitefully used others.

She was ashamed of her attitude. Noah coming to church was not about her or her ridiculous feelings for someone totally out of her orbit. Today was about him and Lili coming home to a loving Father. Connecting with a supportive community of fellow believers. And finding a spiritual home.

At the close of the sermon, Shayla Morgan took her place on a stool beside the pulpit, strumming the guitar in her arms.

Growing up in Truelove, she'd been a year ahead of Chloe at school. Now the wife of a Christmas tree farmer, Shayla had been dubbed the "Songbird of the Blue Ridge."

Perched on the stool, Shayla crooned a song Chloe had never heard before but instantly loved. A modern hymn of praise. In signature Shayla Morgan style, the Celtic-sounding minor chords harkened back to the Scotch-Irish roots of the Appalachians.

Making a name for herself in the country music scene, Shayla was an up-and-coming singer-songwriter with a Christmas ballad that had hit the top ten several years ago.

Right about the time Noah stepped away from that world.

Fear clanged like an alarm bell inside her head. If anyone in Truelove would recognize Noah Knightley, it would be someone also in that world...like Shayla.

Oh, no.

Was it her imagination that she felt Noah tense up across the aisle? He'd stepped away from performing, but that didn't mean he lived under a rock. He had to recognize Shayla.

As the song wound down to its conclusion, her anxiety ratcheted. What if Shayla said something about fellow musician Noah Knightley visiting their congregation today? What if a well-meaning church member accidentally commented on social media about Truelove's *two* resident chart-topping musicians?

Would the paparazzi descend? Would Noah and Lili be hounded out of town? What if she never saw them again?

An ache spread across her chest. This was a disaster in the making. She had to do something.

Reverend Bryant rose for the benediction. Ready to leap from the pew to forcibly block the hordes she imagined surging toward the carpenter, she felt a rush of air from across the aisle.

She turned her head in time to catch the soft snick of the outer door closing behind him as he exited the church.

At the final amen, she stumbled past Zach into the aisle.

With the vague notion of buying Noah time to collect Lili and make his getaway, she fought her way with stops and starts to the foot of the platform.

All the while wrapping her head around a new reality. The Lyric staircase would not be completed in time for the festival. But so what?

It wasn't the end of the world. Nor was the Lyric the most important thing in the world. Though for someone like her, who'd previously eaten, slept and breathed the completion of it, it was a strange, unfamiliar emotion. It wouldn't be easy finding Noah's replacement. But at the moment, the Lyric was the least of her worries.

Swimming against the wave of people exiting the sanctuary, she brushed aside Martha Alice. There was no time for chitchat. GeorgeAnne threw her an odd look.

Reaching the platform, she planted herself in front of Shayla.

"Hey, Chloe." Shayla's blue eyes darted past her, searching the rapidly emptying sanctuary. "I could've sworn I saw—"

"You didn't."

Shayla's eyes cut to hers.

Chloe thrust out her jaw. "Not possible."

"Oh." Shayla nodded. "I see."

What did Shayla see? Her heart beating at tempo *prestissimo*, she held her breath.

Shayla looked at her. "My mistake."

Brandishing a coloring sheet, Shayla's son, Jeremiah, flew to her side. "Mommy, look what I made you."

Crisis averted and her pulse slowing to *adagio*, Chloe turned away.

"I remember what it's like to be hunted, you know," Shayla said in a soft voice.

Chloe froze.

Before fame and Luke Morgan's steadfast love found her, Jeremiah's abusive biological father had tracked a younger, vulnerable Shayla across half the state.

"I won't say anything, Chloe."

She didn't turn around. "Thank you," she rasped.

Chloe staggered outside. Travis gave her a concerned look. She shook her head. But she allowed him and Zach to persuade her to join them and the Hollingsworths at the Burger Depot for lunch. Newlyweds Nathan and Gemma Crenshaw and their two boys found them at the picnic table.

She hugged the cattle rancher's new wife. "Where's Nate's dad and Rascal?"

A dementia service-dog trainer, Gemma and her collie canine had come to Truelove to help Nathan's father last year. Reunited with her first love, she and Nate had fallen in love again.

Gemma smiled. "Miss GeorgeAnne is hosting Ike and Rascal for lunch." She took a deep breath. "We love him dearly, but it's good to get the chance to hang out with friends. And your suggestions have been a godsend."

Although special needs children were her area of expertise, when Gemma had asked for music therapy strategies to calm Ike during episodes of agitation, Chloe had shared some ideas.

"I just wish I could do more to help, Gemma."

The K-9 trainer glanced at her new husband, who was laughing at something Travis said. "Being a family is worth anything we might have to face."

Like the Hollingsworths, Nate and Gemma were a match-made-in-Truelove success story. Chloe, Travis and Zach were the only unattached members of the lunch group. Not that her brother seemed to mind. Joking around with his happily married pals, he appeared content with his bachelorhood.

She cut her eyes at Bridger's wife, Maggie, the rec center director. Was that a slight bulge under the cotton dress covering her stomach? Suddenly, it seemed like everyone was pregnant.

Was Chloe destined to never have a child of her own?

For the first time, she minded her singlehood. Then a mounting sense of indignation grew. Why had the meddlesome matchmakers never bothered to set her up with an eligible Truelove bachelor?

Why had Noah blown her off at church? Was she that forgettable? What was wrong with her?

Later at the house, she was relieved and surprised to find Noah's truck parked outside the garage.

Chloe puttered around the kitchen, putting together a batch of chicken salad for next week's lunches. She absolutely refused to glance out the window toward the garage. Any moment, she dreaded the sound of Noah's truck roaring away forever.

She passed the rest of the afternoon in a funk. It wasn't like her to be blue for long. Chloe was all about making lemonade out of lemons. But not today.

Getting up from a nap, Travis announced his intention to help Noah unload his machinery from the trailer into the garage.

"Noah's unloading his equipment?" Throwing aside a dishtowel, she rushed to the kitchen window. "He's staying?"

Heading outside, Travis gave her a weird look. "Well, yeah. Why wouldn't he?"

The garage bay was open. Noah had unhitched the trailer he sometimes pulled behind his truck. After his identity was almost outed by Shayla, Chloe had expected him to abandon Truelove for good.

What had made him stay? She didn't delude herself into

believing it was because of her. But like he'd said from the beginning, he probably wanted Lili to finish out the school year.

Hauling table saws and other lethal-looking tools into the workshop, Travis was out there with Noah a long time. Sipping her strawberry-mint tea in the living room, she kept a watchful eye on their progress.

Like her, Travis was a gregarious sort. Even from a distance, she could see Travis slowly thawing Noah's reserve. Armed with a tiny broom, Lili did her best to sweep the concrete floor free of the dust the men brought into the shop.

Chloe wanted to join them so badly her bones ached from the effort to restrain herself. But he'd made his feelings crystal clear this morning. She didn't want to butt in where she wasn't wanted.

It was nearly dark when Travis finally returned to the house. Her brother sank into the recliner in front of the television. "Just a regular guy. Not what you'd think."

Cleaning the kitchen, she sniffed. "I don't think anything one way or the other about him." She scoured the sink as if world peace depended upon it.

"Right." Travis's eyebrow hitched. "Anyway, I thought you'd be pleased to know I was doing my part to be his friend."

"Whatever."

Jumping to his feet, he grabbed her around the neck and rubbed his knuckles along her head.

"Stop it." She swatted at him. "You're messing up my hair." Which only made him laugh harder.

Brothers…

"Now you owe me." She pointed her finger at him. "No excuses. You absolutely have to come to the friends' cookout next weekend."

"Who else is coming?"

He grimaced at the mention of the veterinarian. "I'm not asking Ingrid out, Chloe. Not even for you."

She flicked her hair behind her shoulder. "Nobody's asking you to."

Because her conscience hurt about Jeffrey, she told Travis about the text she'd sent to their eldest sibling, inviting him to the cookout, too. "Not that I think he'll come."

Travis shrugged. "Lately, I've sensed maybe he's ready to reconnect with the world."

"You sound like Mom. Hopelessly optimistic."

He smiled. "Who doesn't need a mother like that in your corner?" Travis turned on the tv.

She gazed across the lawn to the garage. A light glowed from Lili's bedroom. Her heart ached that the little girl would never know her mother. Had Noah ever had anyone in his corner?

Restless, she stood up, punched the pillow at her back and sat down again. Travis flicked her a look before returning to the nature documentary on the screen.

Noah Brenden and his motherless child were not her concern. She had a busy, appointment-filled week ahead. She'd see Lili in class, but otherwise, it shouldn't be too hard to avoid her father. Chloe had a wonderful family, lots of friends, fulfilling work and a great life.

She was happy. Truly. Oh so happy with her life.

Really. She was.

Staring bleakly into the night, she slumped against the cushion.

Though she hated with every ounce of her being to admit it, maybe Jeffrey wasn't entirely wrong. Perhaps it was time to concentrate less on everyone else's happiness and give her own more attention.

Even if her happiness could never and would never involve a certain blue-eyed singer turned carpenter.

Chapter Nine

Yesterday, Noah had been stunned to realize Shayla Morgan attended the little church in Truelove. Her star had been rising about the same time he walked away from his. When the service ended, he'd raced for the exit on the off chance the singer recognized him.

On Monday morning, after dropping Lili at school, he went straight to the Lyric to find IdaLee waiting for him at the base of the staircase.

IdaLee volunteered at the preschool. Lili spoke fondly of her. But he'd made it a policy to steer clear of the matchmakers.

Forces of nature, the matchmaking double-name cronies were determined to help everyone in the Blue Ridge mountain town find their happily-ever-after. Whether the recipients of their efforts wanted them to or not.

A category into which he definitely fell. He wasn't sure what drove IdaLee and her compatriots to their matrimonial machinations, but from what he'd observed, only mayhem followed the unfortunate recipients of their attention.

Snow-white hair tucked into a bun on the top of her head, IdaLee smiled at him. Increasing his uneasiness. It was never a good thing to pop up on the older woman's radar.

He cleared his throat. "Is there something I can help you with, ma'am?" A loaded question he regretted as soon as the words were spoken.

"Quite possibly." The octogenarian's eyes, an unusual

shade of violet-blue, twinkled. "But that is for another day." She waved her gnarled hand. "Today, I'm here to help you."

His stomach tightened.

The elderly woman reached into a large bag sitting on the bottom step and plucked out a yellowed sheath of brittle, rolled papers. "I'm passing these along to you in the hopes you will find them useful."

He unrolled the papers to find the original architectural renderings of the Lyric Theater. There were detailed drawings of the newel posts—the filigree, the rosettes and the spindles. At the bottom of the document, he found a materials list, indicating the species of wood for each element of the intricately carved staircase.

"This is a gold mine of information." He grinned at the elderly woman. "I promise to treat your documents with the greatest of care until I return them to you."

"Ancient as I am, even I wasn't around when the Lyric was built." She laughed. "As town historian, I found these in the library archives."

"This will shave days off the time it would have taken me to analyze the structure."

"I'm so pleased."

She resettled the strap of her purse on her shoulder. Something old-fashioned and clean-smelling like lavender wafted in the air between them. "I was also pleased to see you and Lili visiting us at church yesterday. I do hope you felt welcome."

"Yes, ma'am. We did."

Everyone had been far more welcoming than he'd supposed to a stranger venturing into their midst for the first time.

"Wonderful." Like a tiny, pert wren, she tilted her head at him. "I do hope you will visit us again."

He'd enjoyed the service. The pastor had a down-to-earth way of explaining the Bible. But he couldn't risk running into Shayla Morgan again.

"Maybe." He didn't want to hurt her feelings. "Once the Lyric is finished, we'll move on to the next project."

"I think most people would agree Truelove is a very special place."

Not knowing what else to say, he clutched the roll of papers. "It is indeed."

She inclined her head. "What makes Truelove special is its people."

"But like I said, after the Lyric is finished…" Trying not to offend, he shrugged. Had the infamous matchmakers decided to make a project out of him?

She smiled at him, not appearing in the least offended. "Truelove has a way of growing on you. You may find we have everything you've ever wanted."

An image of the meadow flew into his brain. And of Chloe with his arms around her. He rubbed the back of his neck.

"I shall leave you to your work." She patted his arm. "Do think on what I've said."

He did a thorough assessment of any warping, water damage or failing finishes on the structure.

Finding a quiet corner in the auditorium, he typed up a work specification document on his laptop, detailing the scope of the staircase restoration. Including treatment methods and woodwork elements that would need to be replicated.

As he hit Send, Colton clapped him on the back. "The very man I was looking for."

"I just sent you and the architect in Asheville a copy of my plans for the staircase."

Colton's phone dinged with the incoming message. The project supervisor dropped into the seat beside him. "I love getting stuff before I have to ask. What's your next step?"

"I'll tape off the area where I'll be working. Then strip off the old varnish, clean and sand the existing structure. I'll also need to source replacement wood for some of the components."

Colton scanned the document on his phone.

"From a structural standpoint, I find modern standardized lumber at the big box stores doesn't give the same dimension or the quality of wood grain we're after for a restoration. For the sake of authenticity on a project of this magnitude, it'll be a challenge."

Colton put down his phone. "This project is a first for me in terms of historical preservation. I'm learning a lot. Where do you normally source your wood?"

"My go-to hardwood specialty store is in Kentucky. Normally, I'd take a field trip there to hand select the wood I need, but with the tight timetable..."

"There's a specialty store like that over at the county seat. Been there for years. Local woodworkers rave about the products and customer service. You could check it out." Colton gave him the website address.

Bending over his laptop, Noah scrolled. "This looks fantastic. I'll head over there right now."

"Glad I could help." Colton rose. "If there's any chance you'll be in Truelove about noon, give me a holler and we could have lunch together at the Jar. I'd enjoy getting to know you better."

He was surprised and touched by Colton's offer of friendship. "I'd like that."

"I'll see you later." Colton stuffed his hands in his pockets. "Hope you find what you need."

Noah headed for his truck. Leaving Truelove, he took a secondary road that wound over the ridge toward the county seat. *What do I need?*

He'd learned early not to need or expect much. Granddad used to say a man only needed three things for a happy life—good work to do, something to look forward to and someone to love.

During his music career, he had made the mistake of making work his life. Now he knew better. Good work meant ensuring a stable, safe environment for Lili. No more. No less.

Lili was the reason he got up every morning. She was also the one, the only one, he loved.

Had his expectations gone from being too high to way too low? Was there something else out there—someone else—he ought to be on the lookout for? Someone he should love besides Lili?

Like Chloe…

Maybe one day when Lili was older, he might put himself out there again. Not for his sake, but for hers.

It was becoming increasingly clear Lili needed someone in her life besides him. A mother. But not Chloe. She deserved so much more than someone as damaged as him.

At the specialty hardwood store, the tall, dark-haired store owner helped him sort through the aged mahogany he'd need to recreate the damaged-beyond-repair spindles and missing components of the newel posts. Per Colton's instructions, he put the charges on the arts center account.

The store owner smiled. "I've heard a lot about you."

He stiffened.

"Nice to finally meet you, Mr. Brenden."

Brenden, not Knightley.

He exhaled. "Do we have mutual friends?"

"I'm Alan Randolph." He grinned at Noah. "I hear from Travis you're staying at my childhood home."

Of course, the dark hair and eyes. Travis had gone fishing with his older brother and nephew on Saturday. Alan must be a few years older than Noah.

"You're the Squirt's dad."

Alan laughed. "That would be me."

He surveyed the store. "You've got yourself a nice operation here." He gave a low whistle. "Looking at your live edge boards, I don't mind telling you I could easily acquire a case of woodworker envy."

Alan chuckled. "Thanks. I married into the business my father-in-law started decades ago."

"I'm surprised you don't live in Truelove with the rest of your family."

"Love and marriage brought me to the other side of the mountain." Alan placed a calloused hand over his chest. "But my heart will always belong to Truelove." He winked. "Fair warning—single folk don't stay unattached long in Truelove, if you know what I mean."

Noah squared his shoulders. "I've met the Double Name Club, but I'm here to do a job. Not looking for anything else."

"Want to guess how many of my childhood friends never saw it coming, either?" Alan grinned. "Those ladies do love a challenge."

He helped Noah carry the lumber out to his truck and tie it down. When another vehicle pulled into the parking lot, Alan stepped back. "Tell Chloe hello for me."

Noah's stomach twisted. He would, if Chloe were still on speaking terms with him.

"Hope you'll stick around so we can get to know each other better."

Noah opened his door. "That would be nice, but like I said I'm not interested in happily-ever-after."

"That's exactly what those friends of mine said, too."

At his expression, Chloe's brother laughed and waved him off.

He cranked the engine. What was with the guys in Truelove that Chloe hadn't already been taken off the market? He'd had a close look at her sitting with the mechanic at church. And he hadn't enjoyed it. Not one bit.

Gripping the wheel, he followed the road back to Truelove.

In his opinion, the mechanic was goofy. He supposed he deserved the discomfort he'd felt watching Zach—even thinking the dude's name made his lip snarl—make much over Chloe.

Which was ridiculous. He had no claim on the music therapist. But like a dog with a bone, he couldn't let go of speculating if her single status was already in the process of changing.

But with Zach? Seriously...

He gritted his teeth. Not that it was any of his concern. If not the mechanic, then there'd soon be someone else. Which was exactly as it should be.

But that didn't mean he had to like it. A disquieting emptiness knotted his gut. It wasn't like Chloe was his girl. He wasn't in the market for a girl, any girl, much less someone as wonderful as the petite music therapist.

He drove straight to his temporary workshop and unloaded the timber. The house had a quiet, unoccupied air.

After the kiss, he'd been taken aback at how much he wanted her in his life. He was the king of no strings. And Chloe was the poster girl for complications.

He'd tried to be aloof with her on the way back from the picnic. Yet her eternal optimism about people and refusal to see anything but the positive had forced him to resort to more desperate measures.

Noah wasn't proud of how he'd handled things with her. But when she hadn't seemed to get the message, he'd panicked. Leading to a more public brush-off. He'd embarrassed her in front of her friends and hurt her feelings.

She probably hated him. But better she learn now what kind of guy he was before hearts got entangled.

Her heart or his?

Getting back in the truck, he sat there, staring into space. Warmhearted and generous to a fault, she wore her heart on her sleeve. Unlike other women he'd known, with her there was no subterfuge. No guile. What you saw was what you got. She was straightforward with her emotions.

He loved—no, he really *liked*—that about Chloe. She was one in a million. A real sweetheart. Just not his.

Noah banged his head against the steering wheel.

When would he get it through his thick skull, she couldn't be his. She couldn't be with somebody like him. That was the worst consequence of being Noah Knightley—losing out on the chance to be with someone wonderful like her.

Not in the greatest frame of mind, he started the engine. At the Jar, he found Colton waiting for him in what he'd come to think of as his favorite booth overlooking the square. Through the trees, he could make out the gazebo.

Over burgers and fries, he discovered he and Colton had lots in common. Raised in the foster care system, Colton's upbringing had been as chaotic as Noah's. And like Noah, the former soldier had been forced through tragic circumstances to single parent. Yet somehow Colton had gotten beyond his dysfunctional childhood.

Colton opened up about his struggles and the long road back to Truelove where love had indeed awaited in the person of his childhood best friend.

"Life is good." Colton leaned against the booth. "Mollie and my son are my world. And every day it only gets better."

The feeling of unease grew within Noah. Was his life good? He would have said yes until... Until the day a certain music therapist dropped out of a tree and into his arms.

Being on the outs with Chloe left him feeling strangely out of sorts. Discombobulated. Disjointed.

Aside from Lili, his life was merely okay. Not good. Certainly not great. Nor had he any prospect of it getting better.

He walked back to the Lyric with Colton and got to work.

But a general unhappiness danced at the edges of his mind for the rest of the afternoon. And into the evening, too.

Per his new arrangement with ErmaJean, he picked up Lili at her house after work. He made dinner. He went through the motions. Eventually, after a few songs, a few stories and prayer, he tucked Lili into bed.

Restless without knowing why, he soon turned off the television. One day this would be his entire life. One day Lili wasn't going to need him anymore. And without her, what did he have?

No one. Zilch. Zero. Nada. Nothing but four blank walls staring at him.

As a teen, when he'd wrestled against the pain and uncertainty of his life, he'd poured his feelings into the words of a song. Music had always been a way for him to process his emotions and make sense of the world.

But when he'd walked out of the hospital four years ago with newborn Lili in his arms, he walked away not only from the recording contracts and the audience. He'd walked away from the music, too. From the passion that once defined his life.

Going into his bedroom, he pulled out his guitar case. His heart pounded. He wasn't sure why he felt so scared.

Taking out his guitar, he sat on the bed. It felt right to be holding the guitar again. Like the well-worn chisel that once belonged to his grandfather fit in his hand.

Like Chloe had felt in his arms underneath the tree in the meadow.

He ran his fingers over the strings. His hand shook. He stopped.

"God, should I?" he whispered.

The weight of the guitar rested against his lap. Taking a breath, he fingered a G chord with his fret hand and ran the fingers of his strumming hand softly over the strings. He smiled and took a few minutes to tune the guitar.

A couple of notes ran through his head. He looked at the ceiling. Should he do this? It had been so long since the creative urge to make music came over him.

But the notes wouldn't leave him alone. He hummed them under his breath. Words followed.

Feeling a sense of peace, he retrieved a bundle of blank sheet music he kept stored in the case. He began to capture the music in his head then put it down on paper.

When he looked up again, it was late. Far later than he'd realized. But he had the makings of a song. A song about wildflowers, little girls, the fathers who loved them and other marvels of God's creation. By the time he turned out the light, something tight inside him had eased.

Over the next few days, he and Lili got into a new routine. He dropped her off at school in the mornings. He stripped the wood on the staircase and sanded it. He made repairs. The more intricate millwork he reserved for afternoons in the workshop.

He worked at a relentless pace. As hard as he could go every day to wear himself out so when he finally fell asleep at night, he wouldn't dream.

Of Chloe.

Colton introduced him to a few of his buddies, who joined them at lunch several times that week. It was disconcerting to go from loner to finding himself hanging with new friends at the Jar.

Noah worried—an ever-constant theme in his life—someone might recognize him. But if they did, no one said anything. Everyone accepted him as Noah Brenden. Preservation carpenter. Single dad. Regular guy.

He managed to make a few discreet inquiries about the likelihood of being outed by Shayla Morgan. He was relieved to discover she and her family had left for a few weeks to re-cord a new album in Nashville. The coast would be clear for him and Lili to return to church on Sunday.

Every night after Lili went to sleep, he got out his guitar. After a four-year drought, the songs poured out of him. One after the other.

Of Chloe, he saw nothing. Her absence, and the knowl-edge he'd hurt her, gnawed at him. She was avoiding him, and he didn't blame her. But he'd gotten into the habit—a bad habit—of watching for her car in the driveway.

Sometimes he'd catch a glimpse of her silhouette through the light streaming from the kitchen window. But it was merely a shadow of the real thing, and it did nothing to erase the ache in his chest.

How do you miss a person so much after only knowing them for a week?

But he did. Her smile. Her laugh. Her off-the-wall humor. The way her eyes warmed when something or someone made her happy. *Oh, to be that someone.*

Such was not to be his destiny, but the longing to see her, to just be in her presence, refused to abate.

At lunch on Friday, cattle rancher Clay McKendry asked if he and Lili were coming to Colton's house for the friends' get-together on Saturday.

"I forgot to RSVP, so I guess we won't."

Colton shrugged. "I can pass on your RSVP."

He traced the condensation on his tea glass. "It's a potluck. I don't have anything to bring."

"We've got plenty of hamburgers for the grill." Colton shook his head. "Mollie has been preparing side dishes all week."

The young cowboy grinned. "Kelsey, too."

Colton nodded. "There'll be no danger of running out of food. Seriously, we'd love to have you there."

Somehow, without necessarily meaning to, he found himself agreeing to come. It had been a long week. Good in some ways. He'd made a lot of progress on the staircase.

He'd had fun with Lili. Made new friends. The music had returned to him.

But in other ways, it had been a long, lonely week. Simply because he hadn't spent any time with Chloe. A realization that didn't make him any happier.

Since when had she become so important to his well-being?

But if he went to the cookout, she would be there. And for the life of him, he couldn't deny himself a chance to catch a real glimpse of her.

It would serve him right if she snubbed him to his face. Yet even his unease over being found out wasn't enough to deter him from the prospect of seeing her again.

Chapter Ten

At the cookout Saturday afternoon, Chloe was determined to put a not-so-happy week behind her.

Over the last six days, she had made it a point to be absent from the house as much as possible. Anxious not to accidentally run into Noah, she'd decided to be anywhere but where he might be. She felt practically driven out of her home.

She set the bowl of potato salad on the table under the trees in Mollie's backyard with more force than necessary.

Ingrid glanced at her. "Is everything all right?"

She pasted on a bright smile. "Never better. How about you?"

"You're sure I look okay? I'm not used to wearing such casual attire." A pucker between her brows, Ingrid returned to folding the napkins at the end of the table. "I kind of went overboard. Are you sure it's not too much?"

For the get-together, Chloe had donned cropped jeans, a soft lilac T-shirt and comfortable brown leather slides.

She gave Ingrid's outfit a closer look. "Ummmm…" Ivory linen pencil skirt. Fancy and expensive taupe espadrilles. Casual? "Not sure what you mean."

Ingrid's eyes widened. "I've gone totally casual." Her hand fluttered. "The blouse, Chloe."

"Still not getting it." Examining Ingrid's light blue silk blouse, she put on her making-an-effort face. "Yes…?"

Ingrid threw out her hands. "It's sleeveless, Chloe."

"Oh." She hid a smile. "Of course. But I think you're good."

Ingrid bit her lip. "Not too casual?"

"Not at all." She managed to answer with complete honesty.

The veterinarian fingered the hem of her "casual" shirt. "I only want to make a good impression on Lieutenant Bradley."

Chloe patted her bare arm. "As usual, you look gorgeous." If she had Ingrid's long legs, she'd show them off every chance she got, too.

Ingrid's flawless face relaxed a bit. "Thanks. You're the best friend I've ever had."

Her conscience twinged. If she hadn't made a project out of Ingrid, would they have spent as much time together?

In what she'd privately dubbed Project Matchmaker, Chloe had spent the majority of last week prepping Ingrid for her debut to Truelove's remaining eligible bachelors. Mainly, the fire chief's second-in-command, Tate Bradley.

Securing her dog, Blue, in the house, Mollie came out carrying a platter of hamburger patties and hot dogs to Colton at the grill. The McKendrys arrived. Through their committee work on the Lyric, she and Kelsey had become fast friends, too.

Other party guests soon followed—like Sam and Lila Gibson from down the block. Emma Cate ran off to play with Colton's son, Oliver. Lila propped nine-month-old Asher on her hip.

The fire chief, Will MacKenzie and his wife, Kara, came in with their son, Maddox. Then the Greens, the Hollingsworths and the McAbees followed. Soon the backyard was filled with families, laughter and the mouthwatering aroma of meat cooking on the grill.

When Tate Bradley arrived, she made sure to do her matchmaker duty and introduced Ingrid to the handsome firefighter. Observing their interaction from across the yard, she was pleased to find the two of them easily conversing.

Most men were initially attracted to the veterinarian, but once they got to know her a little, that was when the trouble began. Ingrid's prickliness and lack of social awareness often deep-sixed any budding romantic interest. Chloe prayed to-night history wouldn't repeat itself.

Travis walked in with Zach. Imminently likable and an all-round good guy, Zach was everyone's best buddy and go-to pal. Not unlike her, she realized.

No one had ever said anything, but she'd gotten the feeling her family wouldn't have been displeased for her and Zach to become an item. She suspected at one point he might have had an interest in her, but they'd grown up in each other's back pockets. He was like another brother to her.

As usual, wherever the gregarious auto mechanic was, a crowd formed. Ingrid could learn much about amiability from him. But equally true to form, uncomfortable with crowds, Ingrid hovered at the outer edges of the small group.

She sighed. Travis nudged her. Carrying a gallon jug of sweet tea in his arms, Jeffrey hesitated by the gate at the corner of the house. Delighted he'd come, she surged forward to greet him. Most people already knew him, but she cheerily introduced him to anyone she didn't think he knew.

Like Tate Bradley. To her chagrin, the hunky firefighter had already abandoned Ingrid to her own socially awkward devices. But Zach, who'd never met a stranger, was doing his best to make Ingrid feel included. *Bless him.*

She couldn't imagine what he found to talk about with the high-strung, slightly snobbish veterinarian. But making a valiant effort, Zach jabbered on while Ingrid just stood there, a dazed look in her eyes. He had such a kind heart. One day, he'd make some woman a very fine husband.

Midsentence with Kelsey, she was shocked into uncharacteristic silence when Noah and Lili ventured into the backyard.

Across the expanse of lawn, their gazes locked. She went hot. She went cold.

For a second, time stopped. The moment hung between them. The chatter, the laughter, the noise muffled. Everything blurred.

Lili ran across the grass and wrapped her arms around Chloe's waist. "I've missed you so much this week, Miss Randolph. Noah says you've been really busy."

Busy avoiding him. But she'd missed Lili, too. Keeping a wary eye on the carpenter, she kissed the top of the child's silky tresses.

Lili's school friend, Parker Green, called her to come and play. When Lili ran off to join him, Noah joined Chloe under the shade of the oak.

His Adam's apple bobbed in his throat. "Hey," he rasped.

Noah was nervous. He ought to be after the way he'd treated her. But seeing him caused her heart to speed up a tad. "I didn't think you'd be here."

He frowned. "I told you I was coming."

She raised her eyebrow. "You change your mind about a lot of things."

A muscle ticked in his cheek. "I'm sorry." He lowered his voice. "I just didn't want to give you the wrong idea."

"I'm sorry if somehow I gave you the impression I was one of those girls you could kiss and toss aside at your leisure."

"That wasn't what..." He gritted his teeth. "Perhaps this isn't the best place for this conversation." His gaze darted around the backyard.

No one was close enough to overhear, but apparently their body language was attracting unwanted attention. Breaking off from Zach, Ingrid started toward her.

Since causing a scene was the last thing in the world Chloe wanted, she plastered on her see-how-much-I-don't-care face. "You and your privacy issues." But she lowered her voice. "It's fine. No big deal."

She had not meant as much to him as he'd meant to her. Travis—and Jeffrey—had warned her. No need for him to know how much his rejection hurt.

"We're both grown-ups. I get it." She waved her hand in the air. "Wasn't like I haven't been kissed before."

His forehead creased.

"We agreed to be friends. No harm, no foul. The earth will keep spinning. I'm over it. Whatever *it* was."

He rubbed the back of his neck. "I—"

"Chloe." Ingrid grabbed her arm. "Could you help me?"

He glared at the vet. "We're kind of in the middle of something here, Dr. Abernathy."

Chloe gave him a look. "I think we've said everything that needed to be said."

"We're not done with this conversation," he growled.

Chloe sniffed. "Too bad for you, because I am. Done." With that parting shot, she stalked away, her head held high.

She kept walking until she cleared the corner of the house. Once out of sight, she sagged against the gate.

Concern dotted Ingrid's gaze. "Are you okay?"

She took a deep breath. "What was it you needed my help with?"

"Nothing. You looked like you needed a rescue." Ingrid shrugged. "That's what friends are for, right?"

She stared at Ingrid. What an unusual friend the veterinarian was turning out to be. She usually saw herself in the rescuer role, but she was grateful Ingrid had seen her distress and come to her aid.

Chloe gave her a hug. "Thank you, friend."

Ingrid gave her an awkward pat on the back, but she smiled. "You're welcome."

"How are things going for you and Tate Bradley?"

"I'm no good at small talk." The elegant veterinarian drooped. "This is another disaster. I'm sorry for wasting your time."

She shouldn't have thrown Ingrid into the deep end to sink or swim alone. Because she was sinking. Badly.

"Nonsense." She linked her arm through Ingrid's. "You're

doing fine. Zach was a good one to practice on. Let's find Tate again. This time I'll stay and throw you conversational cues."

Together they went through the gate into the backyard. Wishing to avoid further conversation with Noah, she stuck to Ingrid like white on rice. For the veterinarian's sake as well as her own. Such was her miserable frame of mind that she even welcomed Jeffrey's company.

But no matter where she went or who she talked to, she felt Noah's brooding gaze upon her. As the evening wore on, the injustice of how he'd treated her began to build until she was well and truly ticked off. She didn't get mad often, but when she did, *Katie bar the door*.

It was dark when Noah and Lili said their goodbyes. He lingered for a second, gazing across the yard at her as if he had something to say. But with Ingrid plastered to her side like an avenging Viking warrior, he eventually took his leave. To her relief. With little ones needing to be put to bed, everyone soon followed in his wake.

She stayed long enough to help Mollie put her kitchen to rights. Travis, Zach and, shockingly, Jeffrey also lingered, helping Colton put away the extra chairs and tables. Her brothers and Zach decided to make a late-night ice cream run. They invited her to tag along, but she declined.

Chloe was exhausted. High drama did that to her. An innate people pleaser and peacemaker, standing up for herself always left her with a headache.

As for Project Matchmaker, despite a week's worth of coaching, Ingrid still went deer-in-the-headlights when anyone male approached her.

Feeling world-weary, she was the last to leave Mollie's. Tomorrow was another day. But for now, she only wanted a long, hot soak in the tub, a soothing cup of chamomile and some acetaminophen.

* * *

All the way back to the apartment, Lili chattered nonstop. She'd had a great time at the cookout. Turned out she was quite the social butterfly. Maybe Noah was the only Brenden with antisocial tendencies.

He was definitely holding Lili back. She'd be far better off without him. And if appearances tonight were anything to go by, apparently so would Chloe.

A realization that did nothing to elevate his mood. The entire evening had been a study in misery. Due to the chasmic gorge that stretched between them, so close to Chloe and yet so far apart.

He'd had to watch and endure while she flitted from one group of friends to another. Happy, cheerful. After their heated, whispered exchange, doing just fine without him. Whereas he felt sick to his stomach, gutted, hating the tension between them.

And that Zach dude…buzzing around her like an annoying, droning wasp. Orbiting her constantly. Who could get a word in edgewise with that guy around?

Yet Noah hadn't exactly been friendless at the cookout. Colton and Clay had chatted him up a storm, introducing him to the other men. Everyone made him feel very welcome. Running around the yard with the other kids, to hear her tell it, Lili had had the time of her life.

And tell it she did. All the way upstairs. Into her pajamas. Through an abbreviated bedtime routine and a final goodnight.

He kept glancing out the window, watching for Chloe's car. This situation could not go on between them. It wasn't good for Lili. Or him, either, for that matter.

Waiting for her to arrive home, he paced between the window and the couch. Wearing a trail in the carpet, he kept glancing at the clock. Surely she intended to come home at some point. Where was she? Had she gone out with Ingrid?

Or Zach...?

His head in his hands, Noah dropped like a stone onto the couch. He might not be free to pursue a romantic relationship with her, but he valued her friendship. And he missed her.

Noah missed her like crazy. Seeing her tonight after a week's absence had been both joy and agony. At the sound of an engine in the driveway, he raced to the window. A dark SUV turned into the driveway. She was home.

Without the barricades of her brothers and her friends around her, this might be their only chance to salvage a friendship he hadn't expected to mean so much.

He checked on Lili, fast asleep in her bed. Then he dashed down the stairs and out of the garage. When he emerged out of the shadow, she had her key in the door.

"Chloe."

With a frightened squeak, she spun around, the key clutched between her second and third fingers, ready to defend herself.

He stepped into the light cast by the outdoor lantern. "It's me."

Recognition dawning, she retracted her weapon. Eyes huge, she glared at him. "What are you doing? You almost gave me a heart attack."

"I didn't mean to scare you. I just wanted to catch you before you went into the house so we could talk."

She sniffed. "I'm about talked out, Noah. It's probably best we chalk this up to a lesson learned and move on."

"That's the problem," he grunted. "I can't. Not until we work through the issue and get back to where we were before I was stupid enough to kiss you."

Her mouth flattened. "You are a real piece of work." She fumbled for the door latch.

"Wait." He stepped closer. "Please. Can't we talk? I don't like how we left things between us."

"*You* don't like?" She swung around again. "You think you can waltz into Truelove, kiss me and then just walk away without an explanation?" She sputtered. "Who do you think you are? Get over yourself Noah Knightley."

"It's Brenden," he growled.

"Brenden. Knightley. Whoever." She fluttered her hand. "Two sides of the same coin. Same result." She pushed open the door.

Anger licked at his belly. She was wrong about him. He wasn't the same guy he'd been. The old Noah didn't do friendship.

"Chloe. Stop. This is just a big misunderstanding. If you'd hear me—"

She whirled so fast he took an involuntary step backward. *Whoa.*

"A misunderstanding? Are you saying it was *my* fault?" She jabbed the key at him. "That I read more into the situation than your intentions warranted?"

"I-I…"

She took a step toward him. "What was all of that about under the tree then? If this is a big misunderstanding, help me understand." She propped her hands on her hips. "Why did you kiss me?"

"Because you looked…" He raked his fingers through his hair, leaving it standing slightly on end. This wasn't going the way he'd envisioned in his head.

"I looked like what, Noah?"

Not unlike how she looked right now. Radiant. And so kissable his insides ached. Not that he was ever going to say that out loud, of course.

"You—you looked as if you wanted me to kiss you."

Her mouth fell ajar. "Like you didn't want to kiss me, too?"

"I-I—"

"You arrogant jerk. Stop lying to yourself. Stop lying to me." She punched his arm.

He scowled. "Owww."

She might be little, but she knew how to pack a punch. With brothers, probably a learned survival skill.

He rubbed his bicep. "You don't exactly make it easy to be your friend."

"Friends?" Her eyebrows arched high enough to nearly disappear into her hairline. "Is that how you define our relationship?" Her tone had gone snippy.

He rolled his head around to her. "And there it is."

"There what is?"

"Nobody does snooty, haughty Southern girl like you, Chloe."

Clenching her fists, she gave a low-voiced scream of vexation. "How dare you!"

"Yeah. How dare I try to make friends with you? Just like in Colorado, every time I tried to talk to you, you'd put on that polite, unreachable air and walk away. Do you have any idea," he yelled, "how hard it is to be your friend, Chloe Randolph?"

"Because I didn't want to be one of your fall-at-your-feet groupies." Her lip curled. "Why do you imagine you're the only one who gets to control the narrative of this non-relationship? The only one who gets to totally upend someone's world with a kiss and then walk away?"

Noah blinked. "I upended your world?"

"What? No." She folded her arms. "That's not what I meant."

"That's what you said." He pointed his finger at her. "That I turned your world upside down because I kissed you."

A look entered her eyes that made him instantly wary. He took another step back.

"You're not the only one capable of turning a person's world upside down, Noah Brenden," she hissed. "But like you told me once at the Jar, maybe it's time for a taste of your own medicine."

"What are you—"

Launching herself at him, on the tips of her toes, she grabbed his neck and pulled his face to hers. Before he could recover from the shock, she slammed her mouth against his and kissed him. Thoroughly.

Of their own volition, his arms went around her waist. Her eyes widening, she tore her lips off his. Pushing him away, she took herself out of his arms. They stared at each other. His chest heaved.

"Now you know how it feels."

What he felt was the sudden absence of her warmth. A warmth that had less to do with her lips and everything to do with the essence of who she was to him. And how he felt when he was with her.

"How about *that* for a misunderstanding?" She lifted her chin. "Consider yourself kissed by me, Chloe Randolph."

"I'm no good for you," he whispered. "I can't—I won't—stick around, even for you."

Anger blazed from her eyes. "This is why I hate you."

He shook his head. "You don't hate me. Or you couldn't have kissed me like that. I know you."

"You know nothing." A sudden moisture misted her gaze. "Absolutely nothing." Her voice broke.

Her tears were his undoing. He reached for her, but she darted into the house. Leaving him to stare at the door she shut in his face. Leaving him more confused than before.

What just happened here?

Noah touched two fingers to his still-tingling lips. A kiss that not only upended his world, but also left his life well and truly rocked.

His thoughts in disarray, he plodded back to the apartment. He checked on Lili, but with the innocence of childhood, she slept undisturbed. He felt more confused than ever.

Noah couldn't commit to a future with Chloe, but it was becoming increasingly clear he might not be able to live without her.

Chapter Eleven

There was no way to put a positive spin on what happened last night. On what she'd done—kissing Noah outside her house.

Chloe was mortified at her behavior. What had she been thinking? She blamed it on the moonlight and too much sugar in the sweet tea.

She woke the next day with a migraine so severe she couldn't open the curtain. Or face Noah at church.

Travis handed her a pair of sunglasses while she nursed a strong cup of joe. "Hiding out isn't going to make this go away, sis."

"Maybe not." She winced at the beam of sunlight that had managed to work its way between the slats of the living room blinds. "But today I'm giving it my best shot."

Travis arrived home last night to find her alternating between bouts of incandescent rage and feeling-sorry-for-herself sobs. He'd threatened to call Kate Dolan, a nurse at the local women's health center, if she didn't calm down.

"No woman on earth likes to be told to calm down, Travis," she snarled.

But when he took out his phone, she chilled out a bit. Because he was her beloved older brother who cared about her, she was forced to relay some of what transpired between her and Noah on the patio last night.

She didn't tell him everything, of course. Certainly not the part about her flinging herself at the heartthrob carpenter. She'd rather walk barefoot on nails than tell him that.

As he was her protective older brother, she was half afraid Travis might go over to the garage and beat up Noah in a misguided attempt to defend her honor. Except it wasn't her honor that had been attacked. More like the other way around.

She gave a low moan.

Travis's brow furrowed. "Seriously, Chlo. Do I need to take you to the ER or something?"

"Unfortunately, there's no cure for stupidity," she groaned.

He snickered.

"It's not funny."

Far from wanting to beat up Noah, Travis appeared to find her situation humorous. For the trillionth time in her life, she bemoaned the fact that God had seen fit to only give her brothers. A sister would have understood her pain.

Resting her head against the cushion, she whimpered. Travis laughed.

Bolting upright, she threw a cushion at him. "If all you're going to do is laugh at my anguish, you can get out of my face."

Still smirking, he retrieved his keys from the tray on the kitchen desk. "Right."

"Wait. You're leaving me?" She jerked the sunglasses off her head and immediately regretted it. She flinched. "Where are you going?"

"To church." He strode toward the door. "For God and other reinforcements."

"I hate men," she shouted at his retreating back.

Not five minutes later, she heard the telltale rumble of Noah's truck.

Hurrying to the window, she snuck a look around the curtain in time to see Noah reverse out of the driveway. In the back seat, Lili perched behind him.

She allowed herself one more good cry. Then she picked herself off the couch. It was not in her nature to remain down in the dumps for long.

Chloe Randolph was the master of making things work. She could do this. Another six weeks, he and Lili would be gone for good.

She nearly cried again at that less than cheery thought, but she got control of herself. What couldn't be cured must be endured. This—whatever this was she felt for the carpenter—would pass.

But where to go from here? For starters, she owed him an apology. Not something she was looking forward to, but it had to be done. Especially if they were to coexist in a small town like Truelove.

Two hours later, his truck returned. She waited for him outside the garage. Spotting her, his gait slowed.

"Noah…"

He eyed her as one might an unpredictable, dangerous mountain creature. "Chloe."

She peered around him. "Where's Lili?"

For the love of sweet tea, why did he always have to look so good? The untucked, blue button-down shirt he wore brought out the color of his eyes. Although, the skin underneath his eyes appeared bruised, as if he hadn't slept well the night before.

He took a breath. "Callie McAbee from Apple Valley Orchard invited her to a playdate with her son, Micah. Lili was ecstatic at the chance to see the apple blossoms." He shrugged. "Something she heard about from a book her teacher read to the class."

She nodded. "The apple blossoms this time of year are not to be missed."

"Listen, Chloe." Dropping his gaze to the gravel, he shuffled his feet. "Last night was…unexpected."

"I am so sorry, Noah." She wrung her hands. "There's no excuse for what I did."

His head snapped up.

She forced herself to meet his gaze head on.

"Lili and I can move out of the garage apartment."

"Please don't." She felt terrible for triggering a scenario where the man felt forced to relocate his child. "I promise to act like a grown-up for the remainder of the Lyric project. There's no need to uproot Lili." Gulping, she lowered her gaze. "I promise to stay out of your way and stop being a nuisance."

Making a sound in the back of his throat, he scoured his hand over his face. "You are *not* a nuisance, Chloe."

"But—"

"I really wanted to be friends with teenage Chloe. I still want to be friends with the adult you."

She tilted her head. "Why?"

"Why?" The question appeared to throw him. His eyes darted from the magnolia tree behind her to the dogwood. Everywhere but at her.

"Because you're good for Lili. Because it's the grown-up thing to do. Because…" He floundered. "I just like spending time with you, okay?" He jutted his jaw.

A trickle of pleasure ran through her. He liked spending time with her.

"I like spending time with you, too, Noah."

His gaze returned to hers and held.

She laced her fingers together and held them in front of her. "In the interest of clarity, how do you envision two friends spending time together working?"

"Lunch at the Jar next week?"

She nodded. "We'll go Dutch."

"That's not necessary. I'm not a—"

"What else?"

"Ice cream at—"

"I'd love to do ice cream with Lili."

His eyebrows bunched. "I love Lili like nobody's business,

but a guy gets starved for adult conversation. Maybe one afternoon before I pick up Lili from ErmaJean's?"

"It's a date." She blushed. "No. Sorry. Not a date."

Noah leaned against the side of the garage and folded his arms across his chest. "I know what you mean."

Happiness as effervescent as the fizz of ginger ale bubbled inside her.

Noah straightened off the wall. "Look at your schedule for Monday and let me know."

"I will."

He smiled. "Something to look forward to."

She smiled back. "I should probably go do my usual Sunday chores."

"I need to get a head start on a template for the damaged spindles, too." He looked down and then up at her. "I missed you at church today."

She sighed. "I missed being at church today."

"I'm new to this faith stuff, and I'm the last one to offer advice to anyone on anything, but..." He bit his lip. "No matter what the next six weeks holds for either of us... I care about you too much to damage your relationship with God. Nothing else, not even our friendship, is as important as that."

That he cared about her relationship with God was unlike anything she'd previously experienced. She'd seen it that summer in him, an endearing sweetness—usually kept well-hidden—that invariably robbed her of breath.

His earnest desire to do the right thing, to do right by her, humbled her. And at the same time, reassured her in a place deep within her heart she didn't want to analyze too closely. Lest it shatter and she lose this new, precious truce they'd created.

"I am so, so sorry for attacking you like that, Noah."

"You did *not* attack me, Chloe."

She put her hand over her heart. "I was totally out of line."

"I said it was unexpected." He flashed her a quirky, lopsided smile. "I never said I didn't enjoy it." He went into the garage.

The air whooshing out of her lungs, she made it inside the house before collapsing into a chair. She fanned her face.

Wow. Just wow.

Friends with Noah Brenden was going to be trickier than she'd bargained for.

On Monday, they managed to grab an early lunch at the Jar.

Noah was aware of the inquisitive stares of the Double Name Club, seated at their usual table beneath the community bulletin board. At this rate, courtesy of the town grapevine, Truelove would have wedding invitations printed for them by noon.

"I'm sorry," Chloe whispered across the table of his favorite booth. "Maybe if you scowl the whole time, they'll get the message we're just friends."

"Stop apologizing. It's not your job to make everyone happy." He leaned his elbows on the table. "Which is what I sense you often do at the expense of yourself."

"You're not wrong." She sighed. "It's an issue I'm working on."

"I won't let those nosy old women spoil our lunch. I want you to enjoy yourself." He rattled the menu. "Because I certainly intend to enjoy lunch with you."

Lunch turned out to be fun. Midweek, they went for a late-afternoon ice cream when she finished her music therapy appointments for the day.

On Friday night, Amber and Ethan Green invited him and Lili to Parker's T-ball game at the recreation center ball field. Turned out Chloe's nephew played on the out-of-town opposing team. With Travis on night shift, he invited Chloe to ride to the game with them.

In the back seat, Lili occupied herself by looking through

the pages of a book Chloe had gotten her about a small girl and her musical adventures with a violin.

"You don't have to buy her things, Chloe."

"In my session with her class this week, she fell in love with the small fiddle I brought. She has a real ear for music."

He'd started teaching Lili a few chords on his guitar. After she went to bed each night, he continued working on his songs. He never intended to perform again, but he found it relaxing and fulfilling to return, for his own enjoyment, to what had been his first love.

A first love, but not his last.

Noah glanced at Chloe, chatting over the seat to Lili about the book. He gripped the wheel until his knuckles turned white.

He was not in love with Chloe. No way. No how. He couldn't be. No matter how much he enjoyed spending time with her, he refused to go there.

Per her habit, when she turned around, she was still talking. Most of which he'd missed. As usual, honeysuckle played havoc with his senses.

"—Travis will hate to miss seeing the Squirt play. We try to get to as many games as possible. Even Jeffrey will probably come out to support the kid tonight."

Great. He clamped his jaw. Something to not look forward to.

Turning onto Main, he concentrated on keeping his opinion of her eldest brother off his face.

"Most of Truelove will be at the game."

One hand on the wheel, he cut his eyes to her. "A little league game?"

"Truelove believes in supporting its citizens from the cradle to the grave."

He rolled his eyes. "Or maybe everyone will be there 'cause there isn't anything else to do?"

She gave him a look. He grinned. Mission accomplished. It never got old. Almost too easy. Pushing the Truelove button never failed to rile her up.

"You should see how the town turns out for Friday night football at the high school during the fall." She shrugged. "But of course, you and Lili won't be here."

For the first time, the prospect of the next job and the next town didn't fill him with the anticipation it usually did.

As he drove past it, she turned her face toward the Lyric marquee. "You made a lot of progress on the staircase this week, didn't you?"

Between lunch and ice cream with Chloe, he'd poured himself into work. As a distraction. He had a hard time not thinking about her when he wasn't with her. Alongside Lili, she was the first thing he thought about in the morning and the last when he closed his eyes at night.

"It's coming together. I'll probably finish earlier than planned."

She nodded but kept her gaze trained on the passing scenery. "You'll be able to leave Truelove sooner than you expected."

The truck rattled over the bridge, jarring him and setting his teeth on edge.

Just past the Leaving Truelove sign, he turned off at the rec center. After parking, they made their way around the building to the ball field.

Because it was the South, the aroma of fried food filled the evening air.

After giving Lili a hug, Chloe left them to sit on the bleachers with the families of the opposing team. His gaze followed her until she sat next to Alan and a blond woman he presumed to be his wife. Spotting him at the base of the home team side of the metal bleachers, Colton called for him to join them.

Holding hands, he and Lili made their way up, sitting with

the Atkinsons and the Greens. Colton's son, Olly, was a year younger than Lili, but she enjoyed hanging out with him.

During the second inning, when Olly spilled his drink, everyone in the vicinity jumped up to help. Tears welled in the preschooler's big blue eyes. With Colton and Mollie busy mopping up the mess, he volunteered to get Olly a refill.

"Everybody spills stuff." Lili put her arm around her little friend. "But it's okay. Noah will fix it. He can fix anything."

Clanking down the metal steps, he chuckled. It wasn't true. He couldn't fix everything, but it made him feel good to hear her confidence in him.

His good feeling lasted through standing in line at the concession stand for Olly's replacement drink. Until Jeffrey waylaid him behind the bleachers. Scowling, he tried side-stepping Chloe's irksome oldest brother, but Jeffrey moved to block his path. "What do you want, Randolph?"

Arms crossed, the banker rocked back on his expensive loafers. "I want you to leave Truelove."

Noah kept his grip on Olly's drink and his temper. "Sorry to disappoint. But I have a job to finish at the Lyric."

"I should've remembered you right away. Back in the day, she had quite the crush on you. Seeing you at the cookout, it came to me." Jeffrey caught at his arm. "I know who you are, Knightley."

Noah jerked free. "I'm a preservation carpenter, Randolph," he growled. "Nothing more."

"I haven't figured out what kind of scam you're running," Jeffrey sneered. "But I wouldn't trust you as far as I could throw a hammer. I want you gone from my sister's life."

"Your sister is in no danger from me. I'd never do anything to harm her. We're friends."

"I don't believe that for one second." Jeffrey jabbed his finger into Noah's chest. "I've seen how she is with you."

He frowned. What did he mean?

"You may know how to charm the ladies, but I'm on to you. Judging from the tabloids I found online, there was a veritable parade of women after you found fame and fortune. I won't have you wreck my sister's life."

The picture he painted of the old Noah wasn't inaccurate. Shame coursed through him.

"I'd never do that to Chloe. I care about her."

Liar. He more than cared for her. Not that he would ever admit that to anyone, much less her rightly overprotective brother.

"I'm not that man anymore." He stood his ground. "You and your family have nothing to fear from me." He refused to let someone like Randolph run him out of town.

"My sister deserves far better than trailer trash like you."

He didn't disagree.

"What kind of life would she have with you?" Jeffrey scoffed.

"I'm aware there's no future for us."

Jeffrey's eyes narrowed. "One phone call is all it would take to reveal your current location and blow up this new identity you've created. Or perhaps a call to Child Protective Services. How do I know Lili even belongs with you? There's no record you've ever fathered a child. And it's not like she calls you Daddy, is it?"

His heart seized. The guardianship was entirely legal. He had the papers to prove it. But Child Services might not agree his nomadic lifestyle was in her best interest. Jeffrey could make trouble for him and Lili.

The fight went out of him.

"Everything in my business is based on word-of-mouth referrals. The project will be finished in five weeks, and then I'll leave Truelove for good."

Jeffrey unfolded. "I'll hold you to that. Or you'll regret ever showing your face around here." He stalked away.

Liquid dripped between the fingers of his clenched hand. He glanced down. He'd crushed Olly's drink. His gut tanking, he threw the cup into the large trash can and got back in line to get Colton's son the drink he'd promised.

Why had he ever believed he could turn over a new leaf and start a new life? There was no escaping the past. Or the man he'd been. Not when there were people like Jeffrey Randolph out there.

There would always be people like Randolph out there. Jeffrey would follow through with his threat if Noah didn't keep his part of the bargain.

He would never be able to run fast enough or far enough to escape the shadow of Knightley. What was the use in trying?

But despite everything, he didn't regret coming to Truelove. How could he? If he hadn't taken the job, he would have never had the opportunity to know Chloe.

No matter what happened in the next few weeks, he could never regret that.

Because of Lili and Noah, the next few weeks were the happiest Chloe ever recalled.

The mountains around Truelove were known for their scenic waterfalls. Turned out Noah had a thing for waterfalls. Every Sunday afternoon, she took them hiking on an expedition to every waterfall in a three-county vicinity.

Gorgeous scenery. Lots of clean, fresh air. Lots of fun together.

During the week, Noah was working incredible hours to finish the staircase in time. With him not even leaving the jobsite for lunch, there'd been no more get-togethers at the Jar or ice cream.

But she didn't mind. The end of the workday when he pulled into the driveway with Lili became her favorite time.

If Travis was off duty, she cooked and had everyone over to the house.

If Travis was on night shift, Noah insisted on cooking for her at the garage apartment.

No one had ever cooked for her before. There was something incredibly appealing about Noah, a white apron tied around his waist, dishing pasta onto her plate.

They got into a routine of sorts with each other. An easy kind of shorthand that needed very few words. If he cooked, she cleaned the kitchen. She made sure Lili got her bath; he read Lili a story.

Him reading and acting out all the characters in the *Where's My Teddy* series was one of the most hilarious things she'd ever witnessed. She also felt immensely touched he felt comfortable enough to let down his guard and show her that side of himself.

"I knew you had skills, but I never dreamed you possessed this level of acting talent," she teased.

He stuck his tongue in his cheek. "You've barely scratched the surface of my talents."

"And yet somehow, in spite of it all, you've remained so modest."

He made a show of shining his knuckles on his T-shirt. "I believe the correct term is *multifaceted*."

She threw him a sideways glance. "Is that really the best word to describe you?"

He laughed. "I have hidden depths, Miss Randolph. Hidden depths."

More evenings than not, they both put Lili to bed and prayed with her before turning out the light. They talked about everything from favorite movies, food and memories of that summer in Colorado to how they wanted to make a difference in the world.

"One child at a time through music."

"One well-crafted piece of history brought to life again."
They smiled at each other.

She filled her days surrounded by people—Lili, Noah, her
brothers, the kids at school, the committee. Anything to keep
from facing the fact that the Lyric staircase was almost complete. After that, Noah and Lili would leave her life forever.

A smart person would have pulled back from Noah and
Lili. In her head, she knew they would soon be gone. But her
heart wasn't getting the message.

She was as busy as ever—the end of the school year was
in sight. She hadn't given up on Ingrid, either. Going solo
wasn't the veterinarian's strong suit, so she arranged for more
casual outings with a larger group of friends.

Chloe invariably invited Noah to join them. But he always
made an excuse for why he couldn't. With Noah a no-show
these days for public outings, she and Ingrid took to early
morning coffee and strategy sessions at the Jar.

More than once, sitting in Noah's favorite booth overlooking the square, her gaze wandered to his truck parked outside the Lyric. The Lyric was a veritable beehive of activity.
Colton and the subcontractors were working on their final
punch list before the official town ribbon-cutting midweek.
The festival was only a few weeks away.

"You're in love with him, aren't you?"

She turned from her contemplation of Noah's truck to Ingrid's steady gaze across the table. "What? No! We're just
friends. Why would you say such a thing?"

Ingrid shrugged. "Because it's true. I may not be the most
socially adept person on the planet. Subtext usually goes right
over my head, but even I can't miss how you look at him
when he walks into a room." She tilted her head. "Or how
he looks at you."

"I don't look at him. He doesn't look at me—wait. How
does he look at me? No." She shook her head. "You're wrong.

He and I made an agreement. Friends only. I-I can't be in love with him. I can't."

"But you are."

She covered her mouth with her hand. "I am. I'm in love with him."

It felt such a relief to finally say the words out loud.

She squeezed her eyes shut. "Oh, Ingrid. This is a disaster. What have I done?"

"What you've done is follow your heart. What does it feel like to be in love, Chloe?"

"It feels like..." She flung her hands wide. "Like the best feeling in the world and the worst." She dropped her head into her hands. "He and Lili will leave soon. What am I going to do?" she whispered.

Reaching across the table, Ingrid placed her hand over Chloe's. "You're going to do what you tell me to do—never give up. Not when it's something you long for with your whole heart. You must keep trying until your dreams become reality. He just doesn't realize how much he loves you yet."

"You really think so?"

"But you're probably going to have to help him see it." Ingrid shook her head. "Men can be clueless, can't they?"

Wiping the tears from her face, she laughed. "Thank you for being such a good friend."

Ingrid gave her a tentative smile. "I always thought I could be a good friend to someone."

Chloe squeezed her hand. "I'm absolutely not giving up on helping you find the love of your life, Ingrid Abernathy."

And she wasn't going to give up on Noah, either.

Chapter Twelve

It had been a prolific few weeks for Noah. Not only in terms of the Lyric project completion.

Chloe had become the best friend he ever had. He didn't delude himself about the future. They only had now. And he aimed to squeeze every moment of joy he could out of it.

But he refused to allow his relationship with Chloe to progress to anything more than friendship. Instead, he poured his intensifying feelings into his music.

Deeply emotional ballads. About her. About Lili. About the good life, the small-town life in the mountains of the Blue Ridge.

The songs would never see the light of day, but he'd written enough chart-topping hits to know several had the potential to go platinum if he ever recorded them. Which, of course, he never would. That wasn't his life anymore. It wasn't the life he wanted.

He'd been on the wrong path until God and Lili got hold of him. Nothing was worth jeopardizing either relationship. Certainly not fame or fortune, which usually created traps for the unsuspecting. Most of which he'd fallen into and only just managed to crawl out of by the grace of God.

Noah had no desire to return to that world. As a simple carpenter, his life was by far richer in the ways that counted most.

He was happy. Content. A new concept for him. Unfamiliar, like wearing another skin. A life to which he'd never been privy. A substantial part of his happiness and newly found contentment revolved around a certain music therapist.

Spring had burst forth into full Blue Ridge glory. Late in May, the white blossoms of the mountain laurel and the fiery orange of the flame azaleas dotted the hills surrounding Truelove.

Yet like sand in an hourglass, his time with Chloe was slipping through his fingers and coming to an end. Ever conscious of Jeffrey's looming threat, he nixed his public outings with her. But he wasn't about to do without her altogether.

Sitting on the patio behind her house one evening, he leaned his head against the chair cushion. Working the day shift this week, Travis had gone bowling with friends. Lili was asleep in the loft apartment. Noah and Chloe kept an ear out for her.

After a long day, they were enjoying a late respite while nursing glasses of sweet tea. Moonlight bathed the backyard in a silver glow. He mused a bit on the night, the stars, the moon. And Chloe...

There was a song in there somewhere. He could feel it. It was the way his brain worked. A string of notes, a snatch of a melody, played in his head.

She set down her glass with a small thud. "You are a fabulous craftsman and an even better single parent, Noah. I don't know how you do everything you do. It's positively heroic."

His smile faltered. "There's nothing heroic about me, Chloe. Like everybody, I just do the best I can."

She shook her head. "You always do that when I try to tell you what a great father you are to Lili. I admire you so much."

Uncomfortable with untruth, he glanced into the darkness. "I'm not Lili's—"

"You need to learn to accept a compliment, Brenden." She grinned.

His gaze flicked to hers. "The ribbon-cutting at the Lyric

is tomorrow. Lili's preschool year ends on Friday. She and I will be leaving the day after."

"Why the rush?" She kept her tone light, but he sensed the effort it cost her. "With her contacts in the world of historic preservation, Kelsey McKendry could find you plenty of work in the area. Summers are not only cooler in the Blue Ridge, but beautiful, too. You should stick around."

He laid his hands on the armrests of the Adirondack chair. "I don't think that would be a good idea."

"Why not?"

"I think you know why not."

She lifted her chin. "Enlighten me, please."

"We've been dancing around this for weeks." His hands gripped the wooden armrests. "Around us. But I can't stay. I told you that from the beginning."

"We're friends, Noah. We agreed no kissing. No hugging." She ticked through the terms of their friends-only pact. "No touching. Hasn't the last few weeks been fun?"

And, on a personal level for him, excruciating.

"The last few weeks have been…" He scrubbed his face with his hand. "More than I imagined possible, but for a host of reasons I can't explain to you, it's important Lili and I go."

Leaning forward, she opened her hands. "Why can't you explain? You know you can tell me anything."

Noah's heart hammered in his chest. How could he get her to understand? "What is there for me in Truelove, Chloe?"

Her eyes caught his. "Me, Noah. Me."

For a split second, it all flashed through his mind. A wedding ring. A home of their own somewhere in the country outside town with a large workshop for his tools. Lili and Felix racing around a shaded yard. Chloe's belly softly rounded with a child—his child.

If only God would make it so…

But reality crashed against the utter folly of dreams that could never come to pass. His heart constricted.

He rubbed his forehead. "Let's not spoil the days we have left."

The pain in her eyes—pain he'd inflicted for her own good—drove him to his feet.

"I should go check on Lili. Early start tomorrow. Good night."

Noah hurried toward the garage. Before he lost the battle he fought within himself. To take her into his arms and hold her close forever.

He was doing her a kindness. Because if he ever told her how he felt, there'd be no coming back from that. It was a path that could only lead to personal disaster for all of them.

Noah might be a lot of things—most of them bad—but even he wasn't that selfish.

Jeffrey was a jerk, but he was right about one thing. Noah Knightley would ruin her life. Noah Brenden loved her far too much to do that to her.

Abandoned in the moonlit night, Chloe was cut to the quick.

Hurt and wounded, she stared after him until he disappeared into the garage. This couldn't be the end to them. Not after everything they'd shared.

Her heart wasn't ready to let either of them go. Yet how much clearer could he be?

A voice in her head—sounding like Jeffrey—nagged at the fringes of her mind.

He's made his choice. And it isn't you. Running after a man who doesn't want you. How pathetic are you?

She put her hand over her mouth to stifle the sob clawing its way up her throat. What should she do now?

Another voice—that didn't remotely resemble Jeffrey's—

nudged her to seek her heavenly Father's wisdom. But she didn't. In case He told her something she didn't want to hear.

Like to trust God to work out the situation for the best. But suppose His best wasn't what she wanted?

She had encouraged Ingrid to not give up. Neither should she. She wasn't about to quit now. Not when she was so close to a life with Noah and Lili.

The next morning, she took extra care with her hair and makeup. She put on one of her prettiest, most feminine dresses to wear to the ribbon-cutting ceremony. It was a shade of turquoise she'd worn to church a few weeks ago.

From the way his eyes lit when she got into his truck that day, she'd instantly known Noah had liked it.

Why wear it today? She dabbed her signature fragrance at the pulse points behind her ears. Because all's fair in love and sweet tea.

Downstairs, Travis was eating breakfast at the kitchen table. "You okay, sis?"

"Why wouldn't I be?"

He eyed her above the spoon he held inches shy of his mouth. "You seem tense."

"I'm fine." She glanced out the window at the gray, cloudy sky over the ridge. "But the weather… Of all days." The forecast called for intermittent rain showers.

"Pretty typical for a spring day." Travis chuckled. "Even you can't control the weather, sis."

She sighed. "I just want everything to go well for the opening of the Lyric."

"It will. Have faith."

"Noah told me he and Lili are leaving town on Saturday."

"Then we'll have to figure out a way to change his mind, won't we?"

Her spirits lifted. "This is why you'll always be my favorite brother. Thanks for the pep talk."

Travis grinned at her around a mouthful of cereal. She was thankful he was on day shift this week.

She grabbed her purse off the counter. "Have a good day, Trav." She rapped him lightly on top of his head. Their usual sign of sibling affection. "See you later."

"Not if I see you first," he called after her as she sailed through the door to her car.

Arriving at the arts center, she found Noah doing a final inspection of the staircase. A long, red ribbon had been tied from one side of the stairs to the other, blocking access to the Juliet balconies above.

"You did a fabulous job." She breezed over to him. "Just like I knew you would."

His eyes flickered at her attire. Preening a tad, she was glad she'd taken the trouble to wear the dress.

Noah ran his palm along the smooth veneer of the railing. "Definitely going in the portfolio. It's been my biggest challenge thus far."

She fingered the silver earring at her earlobe. "And your biggest triumph."

His Adam's apple bobbed in his throat. "About last night, Chloe..." He stuffed his hands in his pockets.

Then GeorgeAnne Allen and Mayor Watson arrived. Kelsey hustled the other committee members to the ribbon for a photo op.

"Chloe!" Kelsey beckoned.

She glanced over her shoulder at Noah. "We'll talk later."

Camera shy, he was already moving into the shadows. "Later," he grunted.

The ribbon-cutting went off without a hitch. Colton gave the committee and town council the grand tour. Reopening the historic venue was big news among local media outlets. Much was made over the painstakingly restored plaster walls, the glittering chandeliers and the sweeping staircase.

Martha Alice scanned the lobby. "Where is our gifted master carpenter?"

Cliff Penry, the foundation's accountant, shrugged. "He was here a minute ago."

She hated Noah wasn't around to bask in the accolades due his craftsmanship, but given his fear of exposure, she wasn't surprised.

Courtesy of Kara MacKenzie's new catering company, fancy hors d'oeuvres were served to everyone at the ribbon-cutting. The dignitaries and members of the press milled around the enormous vaulted interior.

Chloe went in search of the reticent carpenter. She found him outside on the sidewalk, admiring the art deco marquee advertising the upcoming music festival. "Congratulations. The Juliet balconies and the staircase are getting rave reviews."

She smiled at him. "I imagine multiple job offers will soon wend their way to you. Though by then, you'll be gone for parts unknown."

"Congratulations on landing her as your headliner." He pointed to the big-name musician featured on the marquee. "I did a song with her on a televised Christmas special one year."

"I know. As one of your most devoted superfans, I watched it."

He didn't smile as she'd hoped.

Noah blew out a breath. "I hope the festival turns out to be everything you want it to be."

"The indie band from Asheville aren't well known enough yet to sell out their concert."

He nodded. "It'll happen. They're good, and their following is growing."

Not surprisingly, she and Noah shared the same taste in music. Just then, drops of moisture fell from the sky and dotted the sidewalk.

She frowned. Great. Just great. "But the scholarships—"

"Will end up fully funded. Everything's going to work out, Chloe. Your hard work will pay off. You built it." He gestured at the Lyric. "Now they'll come. You'll see."

"But you're still going."

The rain pitter-pattering the sidewalk soon became a deluge as the skies opened up. She gasped.

He grabbed her hand. "Let's get out of here. Don't want that pretty dress of yours to get drenched on my watch."

They dashed across the street to the square. He pulled her into the deserted gazebo.

She brushed the wet strands of hair out of her face. "I look like a drowned rat."

"No." He took a long look at her. "You look beautiful as always."

He hunched his shoulders. "I'm sorry about last night. I'm even sorrier I can't stay in Truelove, Chloe."

Above them, the rain drummed on the roof of the gazebo. Cutting them off from the rest of the world. Cocooning them in a world just their own.

She lifted her chin. "Would it make a difference if I told you I—"

"Don't make this any harder than it has to be. Please."

She tucked a tendril of hair behind her ear. "Have you told Lili you're leaving?"

His gaze had followed the movement of her hand. "Tomorrow." He tore his eyes away. "After her preschool graduation. She's so proud of that little cap and gown."

"Will I get the chance to say goodbye to her?"

He peered at the sheets of rain pouring down around them. "Saturday morning after I load the truck, I'll send her over to say goodbye."

"And Felix?"

He sighed. "A girl and her cat must not be separated."

"Felix will be a great consolation when she's missing True-love."

He looked at her sharply. "A cat won't compensate for the loss of you in her life. She loves you."

She tilted her head. "Is she the only one?"

"Love's got nothing to do with this." He turned away from her. "I refuse to make promises I'm not able to keep."

She came up behind him and laid her palm against the back of his damp shirt. "Such a heavy weight you try to carry on those broad shoulders of yours. But it doesn't have to be that way. Don't shut out the people who care for you. As Lili's dad—"

Noah swung around. "I can't leave with this misunderstanding between us. Even now it's hard to talk about, much less explain. I never intended to lie, but it was easier to let people assume I'm Lili's father."

Her lips parted. "You're not her father?"

"I'm her uncle. She's the daughter of my twin sister, Fliss."

She blinked at him. "I thought Fliss was your...girlfriend, partner, wife."

"None of the above." He folded his arms. "After my first song went viral, Fliss joined me in Nashville. I should've looked out for her better, but I was consumed by my career. Like our mother, she found herself pregnant."

"What about Lili's biological father?"

His gaze dropped to the ground. "Fliss never said, and I never asked. She was determined to be the kind of good mother we never had. We believed her epilepsy was under control. You know the rest. To my shame, I wasn't there for her. I was on tour when I got the call from her doctor, and recovering from a weekend bender."

"Noah, look at me."

"I won't bore you with the ugly details. I caught the first

plane to Nashville. I had to sober up on the way." His voice caught. "I was too late to say goodbye to Fliss."

"That's when you decided to walk away from music for good."

"What good did the music ever bring me? I was sick of the pitfalls of that life. The wrong choices I kept making. I couldn't allow Lili to fall through the cracks the way Fliss had."

Her arms went around him. He stiffened at the comfort she offered, but a split second later, he leaned into her.

"Thank you for telling me. I'll never breathe a word of what you shared."

"It wasn't I didn't trust you." He wrapped his arms around her. "I just hated to alter your good opinion of me."

Stepping back, she examined his features. "In every way but biological, you are Lili's father. How could I think less of you? If anything, I admire you more."

"It's because of Lili that we have to go. Because of her, we never remain too long in one place." The rain had slowed to a gentle trickle. "We've stayed in Truelove far longer than I ever intended."

She took his face and held it between the palms of her hands. "Why is it so impossible for you to stay?"

"I told you why the first time you asked me to join the preservation team at the Lyric."

"Before or after my failed attempt at blackmail?"

A smile teased the corner of his lips. "The reason I can't stay is the usual issue—money."

"I don't understand."

"The paparazzi are like cockroaches, Chloe. You never know when they're going to emerge or where, but they always find you. They've found me before. Someone is always willing to sell my location out to them for a buck. If I linger here, they'll find me again."

"What kind of life is that, Noah?"

He heaved a sigh. "It's my life. Becoming Noah Knightley came at a great personal cost. A cost I won't allow you or Lili to pay. You belong here. I don't."

Chloe's lips trembled. "Will you say goodbye before you leave?"

A sheen of moisture rose in his eyes. "This must be our goodbye, Chloe."

The sadness in his eyes robbed her of further protest.

"Goodbye, Noah," she whispered.

Her heart breaking, she turned to go, but he caught her hand. "Chloe," he rasped.

Noah pulled her back into the circle of his arms. He tilted her chin with the tip of his forefinger. With his thumb, he stroked her cheek. "Darlin', Chloe," he breathed.

On the tips of her toes, she feathered her fingers in the nape of his hair.

His mouth found hers. Unlike their last stormy kiss, this was tender. Full of both joy and sorrow. It was simply everything.

Because to her, he was everything.

Noah let go of her. They stared at each other for a long, long moment. She made an effort to pull her tattered emotions together. But if she didn't leave right this minute, she wasn't sure how much longer she could hold it together.

Chloe whirled around, desperate to make her escape. A shadow filled the opening of the gazebo.

She nearly bounced off Bridger Hollingsworth's Kevlar-vested police uniform.

Her cheeks colored. "Oh." How long had he been standing there? "I didn't see you."

The police chief cleared his throat. "I've been looking for you."

"Hi, Bridger." She shot a look over her shoulder to Noah,

who had gone as still and solid as the granite in the mountains surrounding Truelove. "Is there something I can help you with?"

Bridger removed his hat and ducked inside the gazebo. "I went to the Lyric first, but Colton told me you might be here."

She must look like a nightmare. She made a vain attempt to smooth her hair. Unusually disheveled, thanks to Noah. "Is everything okay with Maggie and the boys?"

"Maggie and the boys are fine." He took a deep breath. "Do you have any idea where my officer might locate Jeffrey?"

"I talked to him last night. Something about a regional bank meeting in Asheville."

Bridger turned his head and spoke to one of his Truelove police officers.

She squinted through the lattice at the officer, hurrying toward his patrol car, parked between the square and the Lyric. The rain had stopped.

Bridger fingered the brim of his hat. "A deputy sheriff is headed to talk with Alan at the county seat."

"I don't understand." She felt Noah ease alongside her. "What's going on?"

"A little while ago, my office was contacted by—"

She gasped. "Has something happened to Mom and Dad in Florida?"

"No. They're fine. A Florida state trooper has been dispatched to notify them."

Dread, like a cold hard stone, lodged in her throat. "Notify them?"

"Troop G station dispatch contacted me." Bridger squared his shoulders. "At approximately 10:32 a.m. this morning, while on patrol, Travis pulled over a motorist on the interstate for a seat belt violation." His jaw worked. "The first responding officer to the scene thinks while issuing the citation, Travis must have spotted drug paraphernalia."

She shook her head. "No."

Noah put his hand on her shoulder. She brushed him off.

"The guy was wanted in connection with a murder case in Tennessee. He must have figured he had nothing to lose. When Travis ordered him to step out of the vehicle, he shot Travis in the chest."

"But his vest—the bullet-resistant vest."

"It stopped the first bullet, but he shot Travis multiple times, Chloe."

She put her hand over her mouth.

Bridger's gaze flitted somewhere and then back to her. "Somehow Travis was able to discharge his own weapon, incapacitating the shooter. He managed to stagger to his vehicle and call for assistance before he collapsed."

"He's not dead." She must have swayed. Noah put his hands on her arms to steady her. "Tell me he's not dead, Bridger."

"Local law enforcement reached him five minutes later, and he was transported by emergency services to the regional hospital over the mountain."

"Hurt is not dead." Her voice rose. "He's okay, right?"

"Chloe…" Noah grunted.

She clutched Bridger's uniform sleeve in a death grip. "It has to be good that Travis was able to radio for help. Right?"

Bridger's gaze bored into her. "Travis has sustained life-threatening injuries. I'm here to get you to the hospital right away. Currently, his situation is touch and go."

"That can't be right." She shook her head to clear the fuzziness filling her brain. "There's been a mistake. You have Travis confused with some other officer. I'm terribly, terribly sorry for that officer's family, but it can't be Travis." She put on her brightest smile. "You're wrong about him."

Bridger exchanged a look with Noah. "I'm so sorry, Chloe, but it's Travis." He touched her hand. "I need you to come with—"

She jerked away. "It's not Travis. It's not him. It can't be him." She spun around to Noah. "Travis is on day shift this week. This week he's supposed to be safe," she wailed.

"Oh, Chloe," Noah whispered.

This was her worst nightmare come true. How could she fix this? But there was no fixing this situation. No chance to rescue Travis.

Suddenly, the edges of her vision blurred. Her knees buckled. The ground rose to meet her.

And she felt herself falling into the darkness.

Chapter Thirteen

Noah caught her before she hit the gazebo floor. She sat up in his arms almost immediately.

"I'm okay. I just got a little dizzy." She put a hand to her head. "I need to get to the hospital." She appeared more embarrassed than hurt.

He helped her stand. "I'm going with you."

Bridger put on his hat. "You'll get there faster in the police cruiser."

Her mouth wobbled. "You're telling me speed is of the essence?"

"I think you need to prepare yourself."

She gave him a short nod. "Let's go then."

Noah got into the back of the white cruiser with her. "Is it all right if I alert ErmaJean? I need to make arrangements for Lili."

Chloe knotted her fingers. "If you need to be there for Lili, I understand."

He reached for her hand. "I want to be here for you."

"Miss ErmaJean can activate the Truelove prayer chain." She swallowed. "Travis needs all the prayers he can get right now."

He sent off a text to the older woman asking her to look after Lili until he returned.

Twenty minutes later, Bridger pulled up outside the emergency department. "I wish I could wait with you, but the shooter was taken to another hospital, and I'm needed there."

Noah helped Chloe out of the vehicle. She squeezed his

fingers, giving him a grateful smile. At their approach, the ER doors whooshed open.

A pungent, antiseptic smell assaulted his nostrils. The scent brought back unpleasant memories of losing Fliss. He hated hospitals, but this wasn't about his feelings. This was about being there for Chloe. At the reception desk, a twenty-something woman with green hair didn't bother to look up from her monitor.

"We're here about Travis Randolph." Chloe cleared her throat. "The state trooper who was brought in a little while ago. My br-brother."

The receptionist typed his name into the computer. "He's in surgery. I have a note to send family to waiting room three." She looked over the monitor for the first time. "I'm sorry. He was very brave."

Chloe's mouth flattened. "He *is* very brave."

The receptionist motioned toward an open book on the counter. "You need to sign in. Then I'll print your visitor name tags."

Chloe took the pen, but her hand was shaking so badly, he took it from her. "I'll take care of it."

Nodding, she wrapped her arms around her body. He wrote their names in the logbook.

Soon after, the printer rolled out two white, adhesive name tags. The woman handed Chloe hers. Peeling off the backing, Chloe stuck it to her dress.

The receptionist's gaze narrowed. "You're Noah Brenden?"

His heart skipped a beat. "That's right."

She cocked her head as if trying to place him.

"My name tag…" He prompted. "We're in kind of a hurry."

"Here you go, Noah *Brenden*…" She winked.

She'd recognized him. His stomach cramped.

"Can we go through?" Chloe whispered.

Noah put his arm around her. "Come on."

Inside the waiting room, Alan jumped out of his chair. A highway patrol officer also rose. She hugged her brother.

"My sister and Noah Brenden." Alan gestured toward the officer. "This is Travis's squad sergeant, Trooper Dunlop."

The trooper inclined his head. "Ma'am." He shook Noah's hand.

"Is there any news?"

"No." Alan's face sagged. "Jeffrey will be here soon. Mom and Dad caught the first flight out of Tampa."

"The lieutenant will meet them at the Asheville airport and bring them to the hospital." Trooper Dunlop put on his hat. "Now that you've arrived, I'm going to stand watch outside the door. I'll admit only family and friends."

Jeffrey dashed into the waiting room. He scowled at Noah. "What's he doing here?"

Before he could frame a response, a woman in hospital scrubs entered the room. The three siblings formed a half circle around her.

"I'm Dr. Franklin. Travis is still on the operating table. It's going to be a long, complicated procedure, but I wanted to take a moment to talk over a few things with his family."

Chloe clasped her hands under her chin. "How's Travis?"

Weariness was etched across the doctor's features. "Your brother has lost a lot of blood."

Jeffrey squared his shoulders. "Is there anything you need from us?"

"Troopers are required to have pertinent documents on file in case of an emergency. I already have everything I need of that nature." The doctor stuffed her hands in the pockets of her green scrubs. "But sometimes the family doesn't know all the details of a patient's wishes. I wanted to let you know Travis has a DNR in place."

Jeffrey looked at Alan. "What's a DNR?"

Alan shrugged.

"A do not resuscitate order," Noah rasped.

Chloe turned her face into his shoulder.

"This isn't real." Jeffrey looked stricken. "This can't be happening. Not to Travis."

Dr. Franklin fingered the stethoscope slung around her neck. "There is one thing you could do to help."

The three siblings perked. "Anything."

"Your brother has a rare blood type. If possible, I prefer to check with family first. Are any of you a match for AB?"

The siblings looked at each other.

"No," Chloe whispered.

"I am." Noah stepped forward. "I'd be happy to donate blood."

The doctor nodded. "I'll send a lab tech. I need to return to the operating room now." She left them.

Chloe took his hand. "Thank you, Noah."

He guided her to the couch. "I couldn't help Fliss, but maybe I can help Travis."

Jeffrey and Alan resumed their seats. "Who's Fliss?"

She looked at Noah.

"It's okay." He was tired of secrets. He caught Jeffrey's gaze. "Fliss was my twin sister. She died after giving birth. Lili is my niece. I'm raising her."

Alan tilted his head. "That's why you left Nashville."

"Wait." Jeffrey glared. "Do you and Travis know about Knightley, too?"

She straightened. "Jeff—"

"It's all right." Noah laced his fingers through hers.

"Why am I the only one who didn't recognize Knightley?"

Alan rolled his eyes. "Not that I'm calling you self-absorbed, bro, but...after that summer she spent in Colorado, Chlo had every Knightley song on replay ad nauseam." He glanced at Noah. "No offense, dude, but I can still recite 'Sweet Tea, Cut-off Jeans and Flip-Flops' word for word."

He laughed. "None taken."

Jeffrey blinked. "I've always liked that song."

The technician came to draw his blood. After that, it was a waiting game. Reverend Bryant arrived and prayed with them. Soon after, GeorgeAnne arrived with Zach.

Purple shadows bruised the skin under the lanky mechanic's eyes. "Chlo."

She leaped off the couch and embraced him. Noah's gut twisted. It was natural she would turn to her brother's best friend. If anyone belonged in the room it was Zach, not him.

Whatever happened, Zach would be a source of comfort and strength for Chloe. Which was exactly how it should be.

Propping his elbows on his knees, Noah dropped his head. Didn't mean he had to like it, though.

But stepping away from Zach, she sat beside Noah again. Straightening, he eased back. She rested her head against his shoulder.

He put his arm around her. "It's okay to cry, Chloe," he whispered in her ear.

She shook her head. "Travis is hanging in there, and I'll hang in there with him."

He kissed her forehead. "That's my girl." And oh how he wished Chloe Randolph truly was his girl.

Noah could feel Jeffrey's gaze on them. But he didn't care. All that mattered was her. He'd deal with the repercussions later.

GeorgeAnne plopped herself onto the couch on the other side of Chloe. He shifted, but the Double Name Club member patted his forearm. "The Truelove prayer chain is lifting not only our favorite state trooper but everyone involved to God's throne of grace. That includes you and your Lili, too, young man."

"Thank you, Miss GeorgeAnne."

Perhaps if he'd had the safety net of a caring community

like Truelove around him when Fliss died, he and Lili might not have become nomads.

Colton and Mollie came to sit with them. Kelsey and Clay McKendry, too. With any hope of remaining incognito blown, he felt he owed them an apology.

They'd been good friends to him. He'd learned so much about what it meant to be a true man of God and a good father. He prepared himself for their anger.

Instead, Colton shrugged. "'Sweet Tea, Cutoff Jeans and Flip-Flops' was a huge hit with my platoon at Fort Liberty."

Kelsey smiled. "I love that song."

Mollie nodded. "A real toe-tapper."

He gaped at them. "You knew?"

Clay snickered. "We may be small town, but we ain't stupid."

Dr. Franklin sent word Travis made it through surgery.

Bringing a lemon pound cake she'd made, Ingrid was the last person he expected to see at the hospital.

Chloe hugged her friend like she hadn't just seen her yesterday. Feeling a trifle gobsmacked, he, Jeffrey and Alan stared at the veterinarian.

Ingrid sniffed at their reaction. "Southern women show their love with their food."

Chloe's parents arrived later that evening. Rising, he ran his suddenly slick palms down his jeans. It shouldn't matter what they thought of him. He was only passing through.

But it did matter. A lot.

However, the Randolphs were as gracious as Chloe. After Jeffrey gave them the latest information, Ann Randolph hugged Noah.

"I've heard so many good things about you from Chloe and Travis." She smiled through the tears in her eyes. "Despite the circumstances, I'm pleased to finally meet you."

Dennis Randolph squeezed his shoulder. "Thank you for being here for our Chloe today."

A lump rose in his throat. "There's nowhere else I'd rather be."

It was a long, terrible night. As the first rays of dawn broke over the mountain horizon, Dr. Franklin joined them again.

Exhausted and bleary-eyed, everyone tensed. But the doctor had good news. Travis had turned a corner. She was cautiously optimistic about him making a full recovery.

Chloe's parents decided to stay at the hospital for a while. The family worked out a rotating schedule so someone would be there for Travis at all times. The Atkinsons offered Chloe and Noah a ride back to Truelove. Jeffrey walked out with them, promising to return as soon as he'd taken a shower and changed his clothes.

They were in the parking lot ready to head their separate ways when Colton got a phone call. He groaned.

Mollie touched his arm. "What's happened?"

His expression grim, he clicked off his phone. "A sprinkler malfunctioned at the Lyric overnight."

Chloe staggered. "How bad is it?"

"There's a lot of water damage. The entire backstage area flooded." The construction manager rubbed his forehead. "The set is a total loss."

She sucked in a breath. "Will this derail the festival?"

"It took a team weeks to build the sets. I don't see how we can go forward."

"But the children are counting on the scholarship money from opening night. Without it…" She blinked back tears.

"I'm sorry." Mollie put her arm around Chloe's drooping shoulders. "Everyone has worked so hard to put this festival together."

The hits kept coming. It was one blow after the other for Chloe. But he refused to stand by and watch her dreams go down the drain.

"I'll rebuild the sets."

"Thank you for offering, Noah." Her eyes glistened. "But you can't possibly get them redone in time."

Colton straightened. "I'll help. Mollie's dad will want to volunteer, too. I know several other folks with skills. If we work together, we might be able to pull it off."

Getting in the truck, Mollie and Chloe began brainstorming solutions. Moving a few feet away, Colton put in a call to a water damage restoration outfit.

Suddenly, Jeffrey was up in his space. "You're supposed to be leaving town."

He scowled. "Not until I help your sister get the festival on track for opening night. She's poured her heart into breathing new life into this old building for the sake of Truelove's children." He jabbed his finger at her brother. "I won't let her down."

When he texted ErmaJean to let her know he was en route to Truelove, the older woman insisted Noah get a few hours' sleep before picking up Lili for her preschool graduation. Running on fumes, he took her advice and was asleep before his head hit the pillow.

By nine o'clock, he dragged himself out of bed, showered and dressed. He quickly put together a garment bag containing the small white cap and gown. Outside, Chloe leaned against his truck.

She exchanged a thermal coffee mug for the garment bag he carried. "For you."

Closing his eyes, he took a grateful sip.

"Better?"

Looking at her, he nodded. "Much. Thanks. I figured you'd still be asleep."

Chloe's eyes looked tired, but unlike yesterday, the light in them had returned. "I have a graduation to attend."

He smiled around the rim of the mug. "You look a far sight better than I feel. A right treat."

Blushing, she smoothed her hand over the red-and-white cotton sundress. "Thank you."

"No one expects you to be there today."

"I wouldn't miss Lili's big day for the world."

Noah tweaked the brim of her sunhat. The red band matched her dress.

"Hey. Don't mess with the hat."

Grinning, he nudged the mug at her. "Thank you for coming to support her. She'll be so thrilled you are there."

"Just a heads-up." She clutched the garment bag. "Jeremiah Morgan is also graduating today."

He stiffened. "And his mother will be there, too, I assume."

Chloe touched his sleeve. "That first Sunday, Shayla recognized you, but I talked to her. It's taken care of. It's fine."

He blew out a breath. "You've always got my back, Randolph, even when I don't realize it."

The garment bag draped over her arm, she removed the mug from his grasp and took a sip. "Just like you've had my back with the Lyric and Travis." She handed the coffee to him.

"Can I give you a ride?"

She shook her head. "The school year isn't over for my older kids. I need to head to the middle school after graduation."

"Everyone would understand if you took the day off." He looked at her with concern. "You're exhausted."

"Today it's me who needs them." She returned the garment bag to his custody. "The kids and their music feed me."

He got it. No matter how tired or discouraged he was, the music always managed to lift him up, too.

Saying goodbye for now, he headed to ErmaJean's. Through the storm door, Lili watched for him. When he drove up, she waved. At the sight of her face wreathed in smiles, his heart turned over inside his chest. It wasn't only music that fed him.

Lili ran full tilt toward him. "Noah!"

He scooped her into his arms. "Hey, baby girl."

She wrapped her arms around his neck and hugged him tight. "I missed you, Noah. Is Travis feeling better?"

"He is." Noah shifted her to his hip. "I missed you, too, Lili-bell. Who's ready to graduate from Pre-K?"

The little girl raised her hand. "Me!"

ErmaJean joined them. She had made sure Lili was dressed and ready to go for graduation.

"Thank you, Miss ErmaJean. I don't know what I would've done without you."

"It was entirely my pleasure." She glanced at her watch. "But you better get a move on. You don't want Lili to be late to line up with her class. I'll see you there."

On the drive to the school, Lili chattered nonstop about helping ErmaJean bake cookies.

"The cookies were almost as good as Miss Randolph's." Her voice dropped to a stage whisper. "But don't tell Miss ErmaJean I said that. I don't want to hurt her feelings."

Noah studied the child in the rearview mirror. Chloe was right. Lili *was* his little girl. In every way that truly mattered. He would be the only father she'd ever know.

He pulled into an empty spot in the school parking lot. "Lil, let's talk for a sec."

"Okay."

Reaching over, he released the buckle on her car seat. "Why don't you climb up here with me?"

Her face brightened. "Can I drive?"

"Definitely not till you're sixteen."

She made a face, but with his help, she crawled over the seat. He got her settled beside him. She looked at him.

He swiped his hand over his face. Why so nervous all of a sudden?

"There's Parker." She pointed to the little boy and his mom, Amber, walking across the parking lot toward the building. "Everybody's lining up, Noah."

"What would you think about not calling me Noah any-more?"

She turned from her contemplation of the parking lot. "If I don't call you Noah, what would I call you?"

"I was thinking maybe—only if you wanted to—you could call me Daddy?"

Her blue eyes—so like his sister's—studied him. Why didn't she say something? Had he misread the situation?

"What do you think about that, Lili? Is that something you'd want to do?"

Her brow furrowed. "If you are my daddy, what will that mean?"

Noah took her hand. "It means you'll always be my little girl."

"Forever?"

He nodded.

"And we'll always be together?"

His heart pounded. Had somewhere in her little brain she worried one day he'd leave her behind?

"Oh, baby." He swept her into his lap. "You and me have always been forever. That will never change. You couldn't get rid of me if you tried."

She gave him a tentative smile. "So now everybody will know you're my daddy and I'm your little girl?"

Why hadn't he done it sooner? He'd have an attorney make the adoption official ASAP.

"Absolutely."

She bounced on his lap. "I need to put on my hat now."

He frowned. "Could I get a hug or something first?"

Lili gave him a quick hug and climbed out of his lap. "Let's go."

Standing on the pavement, he helped her don the small white gown over her white eyelet dress and zipped it up. Lili handed him the flat cardboard cap. ErmaJean had sent something called "bobby pins" to clip the cap to her hair and keep it in place.

He grunted. There ought to be a How to Be a Single Dad class. Just for fixing girl hair, if nothing else.

Lili raised her arms. "I want to see!"

He lifted her to look at herself in the side mirror. "Good?" She nodded.

The cap slipped a little. She gasped. He flinched.

Setting her down, he made a few adjustments.

Lili gave her head a tiny shake, testing the pins. "I'll have to keep my head very still like Miss Randolph does when she plays the piano."

In the hallway outside her classroom, they found most of the children already lined up alphabetically. Her teacher placed Lili in line behind the Bell kid and in front of the Cox girl.

The teacher herded him down the hall. "You find a seat on the green with the other parents."

Hands in his pockets, he crossed to the square. The Truelove police had blocked off the street for the duration of the ceremony. The PTA had set rows of white folding chairs in two sections in front of the gazebo. On the sidelines, volunteers buzzed like busy bees, setting out refreshments for after the graduation. He waited near the back for Chloe.

Sidling past him, GeorgeAnne Allen murmured a greeting before turning her attention to a clipboard. Like most events in Truelove, the indefatigable head honcho of the Double Name Club appeared to be in charge of preschool graduation, too.

When Chloe arrived, he snagged seats for them in the second row. GeorgeAnne hit the switch he'd installed inside the gazebo. "Pomp and Circumstance" flooded the square from loudspeakers mounted to the nearby iron lampposts.

Octogenarian IdaLee led the stately processional for Truelove's graduating preschoolers. He grinned at Chloe. She chuckled.

Gazes forward, the children marched across the street to the green. The tassels on their caps swaying in the breeze, the class of twelve arrived with all the solemnity of a university matriculation.

"They're so cute," Chloe breathed.

"Adorable."

Under the direction of ErmaJean, each child found their chair, lined up on either side of the gazebo steps. Grinning from ear to ear, the kids faced their proud families.

Allowing for short attention spans, the ceremony was appropriately abbreviated in length. The preschool director thanked the families for their support during the year. She expressed her pride in each child for doing their best every day. Then came the moment everyone had been waiting for.

One by one, she called each individual child to the podium. "Ariel Joy Adams."

The director slipped a ribboned medal over her head. The teacher handed Ariel a scrolled diploma. Family members clapped and cheered as the little girl returned to her seat.

"Joshua Lofton Bell."

The paparazzi had nothing on parents. In the aisle, families jockeyed for position to get the perfect shot of their child's big day.

"Lili Felicity Brenden."

Then he was on his feet. Like the rest of the dads, taking photo after photo with his phone. Beside him, Chloe whooped and hollered and cheered for Lili.

Keeping her head as level as a ballerina, Lili cut her eyes at them. A small, pleased smile lifted the corners of her lips. She received her medal and her diploma. Returning to her seat, she broke into a big grin.

Later, it was Parker Green's turn. How appropriate that the

child born the day the tornado wiped out the gazebo was in the first preschool class to graduate outside it again. Jeremiah Morgan received his diploma, too. After the quick photo opp, Shayla smiled at Noah before resuming her seat across the aisle.

At the conclusion of the ceremony, everyone headed for the cupcakes, supplied by the new bakery next to the police station.

Lili found him and Chloe. They told Lili how proud they were of her.

She took his hand. "I want Daddy to meet my friends."

Chloe looked at him. "Daddy?"

"It was time. Long overdue." He swallowed. "Thanks for setting me straight."

"I'm so glad. For both of you."

She insisted on taking a few photos of the two of them in front of the gazebo before she headed to the middle school.

Lacing her fingers through his, Lili pulled him over to the Coxes. "This is my daddy," she told them. She did the same with the Bells. And the Greens, although Noah already knew Amber and Ethan. But her pride in him being her father and her love for Noah shone in her eyes.

His heart swelled with love for his little girl. He would cherish the memory of this special day with her for the rest of his life.

Others congratulated Lili on her graduation. The Double Name Club. Her Sunday-school teacher, CoraFaye Dolan. Gratitude filled him.

Thanks to Truelove, Lili was nothing like the anxious, silent child he enrolled in school last January.

His gaze followed Chloe's SUV pulling out from the school parking lot across the street.

And thanks to her music teacher, too, Lili wasn't the only one who'd changed.

Chapter Fourteen

Over the next two weeks, in true Truelove fashion, the community worked together to restore the backstage area of the Lyric Theater so the music festival could open on schedule.

During the last week of the traditional school calendar, Chloe was in a frenzy of end-of-year activities. With her parents staying at the house, he and Chloe didn't spend as much time together as before, but the Randolphs always made sure he and Lili felt welcome.

Travis was doing well. He was out of the ICU and chomping at the bit to be discharged from the hospital. There was a long road to recovery ahead of him, but he was a tough guy.

Noah led the team rebuilding the sets. ErmaJean once again came to his rescue in caring for Lili. After several days drying out the area with large fans, Sam Gibson's paint crew refreshed the interior walls. In between shifts at the hospital, Jeffrey came every afternoon to help with whatever needed doing at the Lyric. Probably to keep an eye on Noah.

Noah kept his distance, but on the final Monday before the festival opened, Colton assigned Jeffrey to help Noah with the stage repairs.

As they worked alongside each other for the better part of the afternoon, Jeffrey remained quiet. Too quiet? A silent Jeffrey was a dangerous Jeffrey. What was he up to now?

Like many others, Shayla and her husband, Luke Morgan, showed up to lend a hand. According to Chloe, her childhood had been startlingly similar to his. Their mothers had abandoned them to chase after the fleeting fortunes of fame. Yet watching Shayla interact with her family was a revelation to him.

On Tuesday, they were working alongside each other, sanding a damaged area of the stage when he stopped and sat on his haunches. "I've been wanting to ask you something, Shayla."

Using her forearm, she brushed her blond hair out of her face. "Ask away."

"I've been wondering how you manage to balance your home and work as a musician." He shook his head. "Unless it's too personal to share."

She propped her hands on the knees of her jeans. "I don't mind sharing. Luke is very supportive. Communication is key. Also, mutual respect. And I commit to nothing we haven't prayed about first."

He ran his hand over the sanded patch of flooring. "It can't be easy."

"It's not, but God gave me a gift, and I try to use it for Him." She blew out a breath. "Luke and I decided early in our marriage to allow nothing to be more important than our family."

He nodded. "I feel the same—family is more important than any career."

"The best of my music flows out of my life with them. They spark the songs I write and sing. Luke and I established firm boundary lines in regard to my music. Time in the studio or on tour is time away from them. I'm not willing to sacrifice our family to ambition. Nothing is worth more than them."

He looked at her.

"During the summer, I only do one four-week tour when they can travel with me. After the farm's busy season, I record in one big block of studio time so my guys can come to Nashville with me." She shrugged. "We want another child. The career will always have to adjust around the needs of my family."

"A matter of priorities." He sighed. "You're wise. Wish I'd had as good a head on my shoulders as you when I started out."

"It works for us." She smiled. "By the way, 'Sweet Tea, Cutoff Jeans and Flip-Flops' was like the anthem of my early twenties. Such a fun song."

He chuckled. "Thanks."

She tilted her head. "My son can't stop talking about your girl, Lili. Any chance Truelove could keep you two for good?"

"I'm not sure." He rubbed his jaw. "Ten days ago, I'd have given you a definitive no. But lately, I'm pondering new possibilities."

"Will you stick around for my concert?"

She had an ironclad commitment in South Carolina on opening night, but she would be among several acts performing at the festival on Saturday.

He grinned. "I'll be there."

The next few days were a mad scramble to get everything done in time. Thursday afternoon, he and Colton were the last to leave the arts center.

He surveyed everything they'd accomplished with satisfaction. "We did it."

Colton clapped him on the back. "Thanks to you."

Outside, underneath the marquee, Noah took a long look down the length of Main at the two-stoplight town. "Thanks to Truelove."

He picked up Lili from the rec center. For the last week of their final push to opening night, Maggie Hollingsworth had taken it upon herself to put together an impromptu sports camp for any child of a parent working to get the Lyric ready again.

Big-kid school had let out for summer break, but with the entire committee dealing with last-minute details before Friday's concert, he and Chloe hadn't spent much time together. He was looking forward to seeing her tonight.

She'd managed to squeeze in dinner at the house with her

parents, him and Lili before the festival opened tomorrow. He had enjoyed getting to know her parents. Yet as soon as he'd helped Mrs. Randolph clear the table, he said goodnight. Exhausted from a fun day in the sun at the rec center, Lili drooped.

He gently lifted her out of the chair. Closing her eyes, she tucked her head into the hollow of his shoulder.

"Noah?" Chloe followed him to the door, out of the earshot of her folks. "I feel like we haven't talked in at least a decade."

He smiled. "I've missed you, too."

"Once the festival ends…" She bit her lip.

During the last few weeks, when they had managed to talk, they'd skittered around the subject of his future plans like June bugs on a country pond.

He cut his eyes to her very nice, very *nearby* parents washing dishes at the sink. Then he focused his attention back to her. "Did you say something?"

A teasing glint entered her eyes as if she read him all too well. And possibly felt the same?

He grinned. "You wouldn't by any chance be free for a late breakfast at the Jar tomorrow, would you?"

"A girl's gotta eat." Giving him a sideways glance, she let her shoulder rise and fall. "I could carve out some time."

"Fabulous. Ten o'clock work for you?"

Her mouth quirked. "Cool."

"It's a date."

Her forehead creased. "Is it?"

"Yeah." He put his hand on Lili's back, holding her against his chest. "It is."

Lili went down like a light extinguished. But he lay on his bed in the dark, staring at the ceiling. With so many people in town knowing his real identity, he'd lived the last two weeks in dread of discovery. Yet nothing had happened.

Did he dare lower his guard?

He'd had time to think. And allow himself to dream of what it would be like to stay. To make a new life for him and Lili in Truelove.

The call of the road had lost its allure. He'd been well aware that come fall, when Lili was due to start kindergarten, a more permanent decision would have to be found to address her long-term educational needs. Why not Truelove? He'd begun exploring properties online with the local real estate agent, Mary Sue Ingersoll.

He wanted somewhere out in the country, but not far from town. A big house with a wrap-around porch. A large workshop for his business. A shaded yard for Lili and Felix.

Was it possible, God, after everything I've done wrong, to find a place to belong here in Truelove? With Chloe?

He wasn't contemplating a return to the music world, but Shayla's advice was applicable to any situation he might face—communication, prayer, healthy boundaries. Mutual respect.

Plus one other key ingredient. Shayla hadn't mentioned it because she probably felt it self-evident. And it was. Readily apparent to anyone watching Shayla and Luke together—love.

Did he love Chloe?

His heart jackhammered. Maybe... Possibly... One day...

Noah rolled over. Why was it so difficult to let her into his heart? But he knew.

Damaged, wounded kids grew up to be damaged, wounded adults who avoided emotional commitments.

Might life with Chloe be different, though? Was he willing to take that chance? He wasn't sure he'd survive loving and losing Chloe. Perhaps it was better not to love her at all.

But what kind of life is that? Chloe had asked him once.

As it turned out, no life at all.

If they took things slow, one day at a time, and let their relationship progress naturally on its own...

He'd lay his cards out on the proverbial table at the Jar tomorrow. Then maybe, just maybe, they could make it work. The music therapist must be rubbing off on him.

Noah grinned at the darkened ceiling. It wasn't like him to be so optimistic. On that note, he drifted to sleep.

He awoke full of hope and eager to talk with Chloe. On that June morning, the ridge of mountains was awash with the vibrant colors of summer. He dropped Lili off at the rec center for her last day of sports camp.

Noah discussed future swim lessons with Maggie. He stopped by Mary Sue Ingersoll's office regarding a particular property that had caught his eye.

The morning had the makings of a great day. A day filled with bright beginnings. The sky above the mountains was a perfect blue with no clouds on the horizon.

He parked along the Lyric Theater side of the square to pick up his final payment for restoring the staircase. He spotted Chloe and a newly hired staff member at the concession stand, organizing the candy counter. Catching her eye, he jerked his thumb in the direction of the Mason Jar across the square.

Smiling, she held up five fingers.

Five minutes. He nodded. *See you then*, he mouthed before leaving the arts center.

At the Jar, Trudy seated him in his favorite booth overlooking Main Street. Midway between the usual breakfast and lunch crowd, the diner wasn't busy yet. However, the Double Name Club and their cohorts held court at their table under the community bulletin board. Probably plotting world domination.

Occupying a corner booth, Jeffrey was in an intense conversation with his friend, Jonas Stone, who owned the local dude ranch.

Waiting for Chloe, Noah kept a surreptitious eye on her brother. At one point, from the men's bowed heads, it appeared they were praying.

But then Chloe sashayed inside, honeysuckle preceding her arrival by seconds. And any other thoughts besides her fled.

Chatterbox that she was, Chloe was full of humorous anecdotes about the festival-goers already milling about town and how uncharacteristically congested Main Street had suddenly become.

Trudy took their order for brunch. They were still eating when Jonas left the diner. Looking pensive, Jeffrey remained in the booth.

Noah was nervously working up to getting her take on the possibility of staying in town when Kelsey burst into the diner.

"I don't want you to panic, but we have a situation on our hands."

Chloe set down her fork. "What's happened?"

"Tonight's headliner just sent me an email." Kelsey opened her phone and scrolled. "She's very sorry, but due to an emergency appendectomy, she's going to have to pull out of the concert."

"What?" Chloe shrieked.

His heart dropped. *Oh, no.*

Kelsey handed Chloe the cell to read the email.

"For the love of sweet tea, this can't be happening. She's the big name draw for the festival. Without her to kick things off..."

Kelsey slid into the seat beside Chloe. "We'll adjust. We'll pivot. I called the indie folk band from Asheville."

Chloe groaned. "They aren't supposed to perform until tomorrow night."

Kelsey put her hand on Chloe's shoulder. "As we speak, they're on their way to Truelove, ready to fill the hole in our performance schedule."

Chloe let her head fall, resting her forehead on the tabletop. "They're not *her*. When this gets out on social media—"

"Already out there, unfortunately," Kelsey exchanged a

look with Noah. "Many of the ticket holders are demanding a full refund."

Chloe blinked rapidly. "We're doomed."

Reaching across the table, he touched her cheek. "Kelsey's working the solution. It's going to be okay."

"Things have a way of working out." Kelsey hugged Chloe. "I don't know why this happened. But this is no surprise to God. He's got this. He's got the festival. He's got you. Give Him a little room to work out His plans." Citing another half dozen items on her final checklist, the bubbly event planner left the diner.

"I hope my heart survives this festival," Chloe muttered.

He chuckled. Perhaps this was the right time to discuss his tentative plans. Anything to cheer her up. "About after the festival..."

Hope warred with fear in her eyes. "Yes?" The vein in the hollow of her delicate throat thrummed.

Noah took her hand. "I've been thinking through some stuff I wanted to talk over with you and see what you thought about me and Lili—"

Someone rapped the window. Their gazes swung toward the sound. On the other side of the glass, a flashbulb exploded in his face.

Just like that, everything he'd hoped for, his dreams of a future in Truelove with Chloe, erupted into flames.

A knee-jerk reaction, he leaped from the booth and backed away from the window.

How could he have been such a fool to think he could ever live a normal life? The past had caught up with him.

The paparazzi had found him once again.

Chloe scrambled out of the booth after him. His chest heaving, Noah had a deer-in-the-headlights look in his eyes. Chaos erupted both outside and inside the diner.

On the sidewalk, a knot of photojournalists jostled each other, shouting questions and snapping photos. Café patrons crowded to the windows to see what the commotion was about.

Jeffrey shouldered his way through the gawking diners. "Chlo—"

"This was you!" Noah lunged at him. "You did this."

He would have taken a punch at Jeffrey, but Leo the cook, who'd come out to investigate, got between them.

She put her hand to her throat. "What have you done, Jeffrey?"

"It wasn't me." Jeffrey faced him. "I had nothing to do with this. The way you were there for Chloe and Travis—for all of us—at the hospital, I realized I could never reveal your secret. I would never do anything to destroy my sister's happiness."

"If not you, then it must have been the hospital receptionist." Slumping, he raked his hand over his face. "I'm only surprised it took her and the paparazzi two weeks to track me to Truelove."

Someone outside seized hold of the door. The bell jangled furiously. But Leo managed to grab the door and kept it shut. Trudy locked it. An aggressive reporter rattled the door. Others began banging on the door and windows.

He grimaced. "They'll wreck the Jar to get to me."

Wilda Hollingsworth got on the phone with her son, Bridger. But by the time the police arrived, it might be too late not only for Noah, but also the town's iconic café.

"How did you live like this, Noah?" Chloe wrung her hands. "This is insane."

"What's done is done." He squared his shoulders. "Time to face the music."

"Not so fast." Feisty little CoraFaye Dolan put her hand on his arm. "Those bottom-feeders won't stand a chance of getting past the Double Name Club."

"Yes, leave it to us." Elegant Martha Alice Breckinridge's

blue eyes gleamed. "We'll distract, delay and disarm them to give you time to make your escape."

CoraFaye whipped her long, skinny braid over her shoulder. "They're no match for the Double Name Club, right, sis?" She turned to her older sister, GeorgeAnne.

"If that's what you want, Noah." GeorgeAnne's gaze bored into him. "Dreamers are a dime a dozen. Making a good life a reality is far tougher. Do you want to make a run for it?"

He raked his fingers through his hair. "I have no other choice."

"I think you'll find there's always a choice." Her mouth thinned. "You merely have to be brave enough to seize it."

"There is no other way." His gaze flicked toward the crowd outside. "I have to find Lili before they realize…"

Bleakness filled Chloe's heart. What had he been about to say before the media arrived? She'd probably never know. With a sick certainty, she understood this was the death knell of her hopes and dreams. Her heart constricted. They'd reached the end of their journey together.

This was not the time to think of herself. He was right to worry for Lili. Keeping her safe was the only thing that mattered.

She motioned to the swinging door that led to the kitchen. "There's a way out through the back alley."

Jeffrey held up his hands. "The alley leads to the bank. From there, I can get you to your vehicle undetected."

"I'd appreciate your help." Noah turned to the older woman. "Thank you all in advance."

GeorgeAnne nodded at her sister. "All right then."

CoraFaye fist-pumped the air. "Into the breach, ladies!"

Leo unlocked the door. The half dozen women, none of whom would ever see sixty again, strode boldly into the fray. Carrying trays of sweet tea and egg-salad sandwiches, Trudy and the other two waitresses followed in their wake.

"Who wants an exclusive on Noah Knightley?" CoraFaye shouted.

Capturing their attention, the intrepid Double Name Club managed to corral the invaders. Surrounding them. Overwhelming them.

Once their hands were occupied with beverages and food, the ladies thrust their trusty knitting bags, needlepoint and other projects in their faces. Wielding pointed questions about individual marital eligibility. Handling the press, Truelove style.

With the reporters momentarily occupied, Jeffrey hustled Noah and Chloe into the commercial kitchen. Leo opened the exit and went ahead into the alley to act as a lookout.

At the corner between the diner and the bank, she stopped.

Noah swung around.

"This is as far as I should go." She took a breath. "The two of you will be less likely to attract their attention."

"I never wanted this to happen," he rasped, his face stricken. "I'm sorry."

Noah reached for her, but hugging the brick wall, she shied away from him. He mustn't touch her. Not if she meant to let them go.

"Tell Lili goodbye for me." She lifted her chin. "Make a wonderful life for yourself, Noah Brenden."

His eyes caught hers and held.

For a split second, she thought—she hoped—he might change his mind.

But he swallowed. "You, too. Chloe Randolph."

Jeffrey put a hand on his shoulder. "If you're going to make it, it has to be now."

Wrenching his gaze away, Noah turned and headed down the alley after Jeffrey.

Her vision blurred. A sob caught in her throat. He was gone.

Chloe's heart shattered into a million pieces.

Chapter Fifteen

Darting and dodging, Jeffrey managed to get Noah to the other side of the square to his truck parked outside the Lyric.

The Double Name Club continued to frustrate the photojournalists hot on his trail. They couldn't hold them off forever, but it would be enough time for him to make his escape and get to Lili.

He thrust out his hand to Chloe's brother. "Thank you."

Jeffrey shook his hand, but his dark eyes were shadowed. "Is there anything I could do to convince—"

"There isn't."

Jeffrey sighed. "She'll be so devastated, man."

"She's strong. She has her family." He spared the theater a last fond glance. "The avalanche of negative publicity will ruin the festival before it even begins."

Jeffrey nodded. "We've survived worse. We'll make it through this, too."

"But if those vipers managed to get a picture of Chloe with me..."

The banker's eyebrow rose. "Ever seen what sweet tea can do to the inside of a camera?" He chuckled. "Accidentally on purpose, of course."

Noah's mouth dropped. "They wouldn't?"

Jeffrey grinned. "They absolutely would. Truelove takes care of its own. Which includes you and Lili, too."

Noah got into his truck. Going the long way around the square, he pulled out on the opposite end of Main. In his rearview mirror, he spotted Bridger and his officers arrive to disperse the press.

At Chloe's house, he steered around to the garage so his truck couldn't be spotted from the street. He was thankful the Randolphs were visiting Travis at the hospital. The goodbyes would have been painful.

Dashing into the garage, he bypassed his tools in the workshop without so much as a second glance. Everything could be replaced.

Upstairs, Felix twined around his ankles. He deposited the tuxedo cat into the carrier. Felix yowled in protest, but Noah had no time to coax him inside. It wouldn't take long to pack their clothes. Then, before anyone was the wiser, he'd get Lili from the rec center and leave Truelove forever.

On his way out of the door once again, he grabbed the cat carrier. He paused at the top of the stairs to make sure he hadn't left anything irreplaceable behind. But the only thing irreplaceable he was leaving was Chloe.

Noah couldn't think about her right now. If he did, he'd never be able to walk away.

His hand on the truck door, he took one last look at where, for a brief space of time, he and Lili had both been happy.

This was it. Once he left, he'd never be able to return. Not without the risk of running into Chloe.

He wanted every happiness for her, but he wouldn't be able to bear seeing her in the arms of someone else.

Better to not look back. Better to face forward and start over. Again.

Unable to drive through town to reach the rec center, he took a more circuitous route. Inside the carrier, Felix sank into a sullen silence. Noah kept a watch on the rearview mirror to make sure no one was following him.

Sticking to secondary mountain roads, higher and higher,

he climbed. Images pummeled his brain. Of meadow picnics. Country churches. Gazebos in the rain.

And the terrible look in Chloe's eyes when he walked away.

He made it as far as the overlook on the peak of the mountain.

Wrenching the wheel, he veered into the pullout and just sat there, his heart in tatters.

He put the truck in Park and let the engine idle.

Was it for Lili's sake he continued to run, or for his own? Keeping love at arm's length before love had the chance to abandon him. *Isn't Chloe better off without me? God, what should I do?*

In the valley below, the silvery glint of the river, older than the mountains, curved around the sleepy little town like an embrace. A patchwork kingdom of green forests, apple orchards and the best people he'd ever known.

At that moment, an incredible feeling of peace stole over him. Everything he wanted was in Truelove. The life he wanted for him and Lili was worth fighting for.

Instead of running from his past, it was time he ran toward his future.

He had to save the festival for Chloe. Was it possible for Noah Knightley and Noah Brenden to coexist? He wasn't the same man. With God, friends and Truelove on his side, he wouldn't make the same mistakes he'd made before.

Already halfway to the county seat, he made a quick stop at the hospital. He encountered Chloe's parents in the parking lot getting ready to head to Alan's. He got out of the truck.

"Travis is about to drive the nurses bonkers wanting his release papers." Ann Randolph gave him a hug. "The doctor is evaluating him now."

"What's going on?" Dennis Randolph's sharp eyes took in the truck, packed with Noah's possessions. "Is everything okay with you, son?"

He gave them the short version of what had gone down in Truelove that morning.

"I'm going to be completely honest with you. Ninety percent of everything you may have read about me is true, but I'm not that man anymore. I'd like to ask for your blessing before I ask your daughter to marry me."

Mrs. Randolph studied him. "Do you love her, Noah?"

"With my whole heart."

Chloe's parents exchanged a look.

Mrs. Randolph's eyes watered. "We would be so happy to welcome you and Lili into our family."

Including Lili meant more to him than he could ever express.

"There's just one thing." Mr. Randolph scratched his head. "Have you told Chloe you love her?"

"Not yet." He took a breath. "But I will. Tonight." He outlined for them the plan that had come to him at the overlook.

Dennis Randolph gave him a slow nod. "To pull this off, you're going to need the matchmakers."

Chloe's mother put him on the phone with GeorgeAnne.

"Glad to hear you've come to your senses," the older woman crowed.

"Yes, ma'am."

When confronted with a force of nature like the Double Name Club—or Chloe—he'd learned it was better to just nod and agree.

GeorgeAnne promised to sort out the situation with Lili and rally the troops. "You just do what you do best on your end."

Taking his leave of the Randolphs, he promised to keep them in the loop.

Returning to the house, he had a lot of other calls to make. First, to his financial advisor in order to transfer the necessary funds into the Truelove bank. Then, to the manager of the folk band to inquire if they would be willing to play backup for him.

"Open for Noah Knightley?" The woman gushed. "Are you kidding? We'd be thrilled. This is the opportunity of a lifetime for us."

He emailed the sheet music and arranged to meet for a quick tech rehearsal onstage with the band at four o'clock.

The next batch of calls were trickier—to the journalists he'd recognized on the sidewalk earlier. He promised them one-on-one, day-after interviews if they helped him get the word out to the public about the festival.

Noah also contacted Kelsey, the festival's marketing-publicity director.

"One night only. Noah Knightley in concert. The Lyric Arts Center." She scribbled as they spoke. "I'll get that out ASAP to the social media sites." She sighed. "Thank you, Noah, for doing this. This will save the festival."

By three o'clock, he'd done everything he could think of to make opening night a success. He prayed the public would welcome Noah Knightley's return. He was about to meet the band for the rehearsal when Zach's automotive shop truck pulled next to the garage.

What now?

Ingrid hopped out of the passenger seat. "GeorgeAnne tasked me with Lili duty this evening."

The mechanic rolled down his window. "So far, Lili's connection to you has not leaked."

Ingrid nodded. "We're headed to get Lili and then to the clinic to visit the kittens Zach rescued from the side of the road this morning."

"Thanks for doing this." He blew out a breath. "If the evening goes as I hope with Chloe…"

"No worries." Zach leaned out the window. "The girl is so in love with you, dude. This will be epic, man. Epic."

He didn't care about epic. He just wanted a happily-ever-after with the woman of his dreams.

Per his agreement with the press, he was able to slip into Truelove unbothered. The rehearsal and sound check went well.

He was getting into what he thought of as his performance attire—black jeans, cowboy boots, a blue V-neck T-shirt and a Stetson—when Jeffrey showed up backstage.

Noah glanced behind Jeffrey. "Where's your sister? Has she taken her seat yet?"

"Um...no. Not yet." Jeffrey fidgeted. "At present, her current location is unknown."

His heart thudded. "But she's coming, isn't she? Chloe will be here soon?"

"I'm on it. She'll be in the designated spot per the plan by the time the curtain rises. Trust me." Jeffrey squared his chin. "What you did today for her kids..."

He looked at Chloe's oldest brother. "I'll do everything in my power not to ruin her life. You have my word."

"I'm not worried." The banker clasped Noah's hand. "You're going to make her life, brother."

A lump rose in his throat. He had a strong suspicion he and Jeffrey were going to become the best of friends.

"You've got that backward," Noah's voice rasped. "She's going to make mine."

Turning off her phone, Chloe spent the majority of the day hiding out in the empty music studio on the second floor of the Lyric.

With her professional and personal dreams in ashes, she couldn't face the disappointment of the other committee members. She wasn't up for pretending everything was A-OK when nothing was okay.

Hunkering in the soundproof room, she had plenty of time to reflect on what brought her to this point.

It made her sick to her stomach to think of the promises she'd made to her kids regarding the arts center. Her promises to the town. Her plans were in ruins.

Perhaps that was the real problem. Had she bothered to take any of those plans to God?

She was forced to examine her pride, her need to be in control of every situation. How dare she imagine herself qualified to be anyone's fixer? Anyone's rescuer.

Even if she didn't understand it, God's plan would prove far better than anything she could imagine. She might not be able to see His hand at work in this situation, but one day she would. In the meantime, she needed to trust His heart for her.

That was what real faith was truly about. Not the pie in the sky version she'd been playing at her whole life.

As for Noah?

Her back to the wall, she slid to the floor and drew her knees to her chest. Her heart shattered, she sobbed. It would be a long, long time before she got over losing Noah and Lili.

"I'm so sorry, God," she whispered. "For not trusting You with everything."

She surrendered her plans and her future, whatever they might be, to the One to whom she should have given them first.

The door swung open.

Her mother propped her hands on her ample hips. "What are you doing sitting here in the dark? We've been looking everywhere for you."

Scrambling to her feet, she swiped at her eyes. "I didn't mean to worry anyone." She took her cell out of her pocket. Her eyes widened. She'd missed a dozen calls and as many texts, too.

Her mother removed the phone from her hand.

"Wait. Mom. I was—"

"No time for that now. You don't want to be late for the opening. You're not even dressed yet."

"I'm going to give the concert tonight a pass."

Her mother lifted her chin. "You started this festival, and you're going to be there to see it through to its conclusion."

Chloe gaped at her mother. "But I can't."

Seizing her arm, her mother dragged her down the corridor to the ballet studio.

"What are you— Why are we—"

"If your brother can rouse himself from his hospital bed to attend tonight's benefit, you can certainly find it in yourself to be there by his side."

"Travis is out of the hospital? Isn't it too soon?"

Her mother folded her arms. "He was determined to be here to support you. Surely you can do the same for him."

Chloe's mouth tightened. "Why are we outside the ballet studio?"

Her mother flung open the door. "Because we need the mirrors for Mollie to work her magic." She shoved Chloe inside.

"For the love of sweet tea—"

Mollie raised a pink makeup bag, remarkably similar to the one in Chloe's bathroom at home.

She scowled. "Is this an intervention?"

Ignoring her, her mother unzipped a garment bag and took out a mauve, flutter-sleeve, skim-the-knee dress.

She slumped. "What's the point?"

Her mother laid the dress across a chair. "You don't want to disappoint everyone who worked so hard to make this night happen." She put her arm around Chloe's shoulders. "We just want to make sure you look your best for a night you'll never forget."

Accepting the inevitable, Chloe slipped into the dress and

sat down in front of the floor-length mirror to let Mollie fix her hair and makeup.

Standing behind her, Mollie surveyed her handiwork. "No one could ever tell you've been crying."

Chloe tilted her head, getting a look at the updo Mollie had fashioned. "But I'm still crying on the inside."

Her mother's mouth twitched. Why did her family always find her crises so hilarious?

"Right." Mollie whisked off the cape. "Off you go."

"Pretty as a picture." Offering his arm, her father stood at the door. "Shall we, baby girl?"

"Am I missing something here?"

Her father placed her hand in the crook of his arm. "You're not going to miss anything, honey."

They got into the elevator. Her mom gave her an affectionate squeeze. When the doors opened again, Chloe was even more mystified to find Jeffrey on the other side.

She frowned. "Why are we getting off on the mezzanine floor?"

Jeffrey ushered them toward one of two private boxes. A holdover from the Lyric's vaudeville days, the box seats had the best sightline to the stage.

"Don't tell me the VIP who bought these seats wanted a refund, too." She stopped outside the curtained entrance. "Is the auditorium going to be empty for tonight's concert?"

"Everything is going to be fabulous." Jeffrey drew her through. "The concert's sold-out."

She put her hand over her heart. "Oh, thank You, God. But I still don't understand why we're going to sit—"

Jeffrey heaved a sigh. "Because the same anonymous donor who wrote a check this afternoon to fully endow the scholarship fund is the same person who bought these seats for another very important person."

"Who?"

"You." Jeffrey rolled his eyes. "Stop trying to microman-age, sit down and enjoy yourself."

At the front row of seats overlooking the auditorium, Travis waited for her.

"What are you doing out of the hospital?" She sank down beside him. "Should you be here? Are you feeling up to this?"

Her brother appeared thinner, but his dark eyes danced with mischief. "How about a hug for your favorite brother before you begin the interrogation?"

She gave him a careful, gentle hug.

In the row behind them, someone touched her shoulder. "Sorry to burst your bubble, Travis, but I'm actually her favorite brother." Alan, his wife, Bekki, and the Squirt grinned at her.

"Wrong as usual." Jeffrey dropped into the seat on the end beside her. "I'm her favorite brother." Her mom and dad shuffled past Alan to seats beside the Squirt.

It meant so much her family had come to support her.

Jeffrey patted her leg. "I'm so proud of you, Chlo."

Staring at him, she wanted to ask what he'd done with the real Jeffrey, but she decided not to ruin the moment. It was a bad wind that never changed.

In the auditorium, people made their way to their seats. There was an air of excitement. A buzz she couldn't quite place, but she was glad, so glad the musicians wouldn't be playing to an empty house.

When the lights dimmed, the MC came onstage to the lone microphone in front of the floodlights. A twinkle in the older man's eyes, he promised the crowd a night no one would ever forget. The audience burst into applause.

"Now for the moment you've all been waiting for." The announcer cut his gaze stage right. "Ladies and gentlemen, for one night only...and only in Truelove..." His arm swept the stage. "I give you, Noah Knightley."

She gasped.

His guitar hanging from a strap across his chest, Noah walked onto the stage.

The crowd broke into wild cheers. The indie folk band took their places behind him.

What had he done? In one fell swoop, he'd demolished his secret identity. And he'd surrendered it for her.

Even from a distance, she could tell the enthusiasm of his fans caught him off guard. On his features, she read a touch of bewilderment, gratitude and yet also a dawning excitement.

"Thank you. Thank you so much." Speaking into the microphone, he held up his hand and the crowd quieted. "I'd like to dedicate this first song to a girl I met a long time ago who inspired me. After all, who doesn't love a glass of sweet tea?"

Her heart nearly stopped. The song—his greatest hit—he'd been thinking about her when he wrote it?

For a second across the darkness, his gaze found her, then he focused on the audience again. That special gift of his—making every person feel he was singing only to them.

"Maybe some of you remember this old song of mine?"

They responded with a roar of approval.

He grinned. That crooked, knee-buckling, legendary Knightley charm of his.

At the opening bars of "Sweet Tea, Cutoff Jeans and Flip-Flops," the crowd went wild. He'd lost none of his incredible stage presence. Nor the sheer charisma that was Noah Knightley.

Despite the way he'd lived his off-stage life, the music he'd crafted had always been clean, fun, foot-stomping music. The kind of songs that made a person glad to be alive.

Sitting forward on the edge of her seat, she put her hand to her throat, swept along with everyone else on the musical journey that was Noah at his finest.

"Like a glass of sweet tea... Like a pair of cutoff jeans... Like the girl wearing flip-flops I hope will love me..."

With the bridge—the climax—of the song coming, she waited with bated breath for that one note. The high point of the lyrical phrase—that gorgeous, exquisite note—and he nailed it. With a dizzying ease that sounded like he'd been doing this every day for the last four years instead of nailing boards together.

The crowd exploded in the joy of nostalgia. Tears rolled unchecked down her cheeks. That golden, smooth-like-honey, mellow-with-a-hint-of-gravel baritone of his. The inimitable Noah Knightley.

When the song wound down to its glorious conclusion, he and the band segued into another of his greatest hits. Song after song. The crowd was jazzed.

After a while, he carried them to a quieter place. The noise died down. "Would it be all right if I play a few new songs that have been rattling around in my head lately?"

Of course, it was a foregone conclusion they couldn't get enough of Noah Knightley.

He smiled. "I call this one 'Honeysuckle Summer.'"

Listening to him croon lyrics about meadows and picnics and waterfalls, she sat back in her chair. The next one was almost as fun as "Sweet Tea." About a girl who fell out of a tree and into his heart. He was telling their story—a love story—in the song.

A spotlight bathed him in a soft glow. "I hope you'll like this one as much as I do." Strumming his guitar, his gaze found where she sat in the mezzanine and never faltered.

"I know a girl who's a hopeless romantic... With her heart in her eyes she believes in faith from above and happily-ever-after love..."

She placed her hands atop the railing. Was this really happening? Happening to her?

"Now I'm a romantic, too..." He sang with his heart in his eyes. *"'Cause I'm hopelessly in love with you."*

It might have been the most achingly romantic song she'd ever heard.

"He's singing about you, sis," Travis whispered in her ear. "With the stars and the moon in his eyes like you deserve."

"I've got one final song to sing before I let my good friends here amaze you with their talent." Noah motioned behind him to the band. "I know you'll treat them as well as you've treated me."

He fingered a soft, poignant chord. "This one I call, 'The Rest of My Life.'"

A country house. A white picket fence. A little girl. And spending the rest of his life kissing his true love under the canopy of a tree.

He finished to thunderous applause. Easing out from under the guitar strap, he took a bow. "If you'll excuse me," he said. "I have a pressing engagement with the love of my life." He exited and the folk band took center stage.

Did this mean what she hoped?

Rising, Jeffrey offered her his hand.

"Go on." Travis urged. "I think there's a carpenter who's dying to talk to you."

Her sister-in-law smiled. Her mother appeared radiant. The Squirt waggled his fingers at her. Her dad wept happy tears.

She loved her family so, so much.

At the curtain, Jeffrey kissed her cheek. "Be happy, Chloe."

The Double Name Club waited for her on the other side of the curtain. Eyes shining, ErmaJean, IdaLee and GeorgeAnne beamed at her.

"One question," she asked GeorgeAnne. "Why did y'all never try to make a match for me?"

"Because every once in a very long while, there exists someone who doesn't need our assistance." GeorgeAnne gave her the fondest of smiles. "Someone able to fashion the most exquisite of matches—a love story all on her own."

She clasped the older woman's hand.

"Chloe Isabella Randolph." ErmaJean nudged her toward one of the Juliet balconies. "It's time for your happily-ever-after."

She found herself alone on the balcony. Below, the opulent lobby was deserted. But halfway up the grand staircase stood Noah, minus the hat and guitar.

Chloe's breath hitched.

"How could you afford this?" Her arm swept behind her. "The seats. The scholarship fund."

"Do you know how many times a day a DJ somewhere in this country plays 'Sweet Tea' on the radio, or somebody downloads that one song?" He peered at her. "Every single time, my bank account goes *ka-ching*."

He put his boot on the step above him. "I've tried telling you for months I wasn't a pauper." He opened his hands. "Do you believe me now?"

She blinked rapidly. "I thought you hated Juliet balconies."

"You made a believer out of me." He grinned. "Turns out Juliet balconies are soooo romantic."

She laughed.

"I figured a place like this—a moment like this—requires a certain level of drama, don't you?"

She knotted her hands in front of her. "Why did you come back, Noah?"

"For you. Only for you."

Chloe's mouth trembled. *Oh, God, thank You.*

"ErmaJean told me home is wherever the ones we love the most are found." He held her gaze. "Turns out for me that's Truelove."

"What about Knightley?"

"I've retired the hat for good, except for the occasional charity concert. Like if the children's arts center fund needs a yearly boost."

"To hear you sing… It was so wonderful to see you on stage again."

"I may be exchanging a mic for a hammer, but somehow I don't think I'll ever give up making music entirely. I'm wide open to bedtime songs with Lili." Noah swallowed. "And love songs by moonlight."

She held out her hand for him. In three strides, he was next to her on the balcony.

He took her into his arms. "I love you, Chloe."

"I love you, too, Noah."

He looked at her with those oh-so-blue eyes of his. "I think I've loved you for a long time, but I've been too afraid to admit it."

"Maybe since a girl fell out of a tree and into your heart?"

"Perhaps even before then. After Fliss died, I wonder if the wandering was me trying to find a way to you. To the girl in whose eyes I beheld the man I wanted to be."

She pressed her forehead against his. "You are the one I've loved forever."

"Will you marry me, Chloe?"

She kissed him. "Yes."

Before she knew what was happening, he swept her off her feet.

"She said yes!" he hollered over the balcony.

Cheers broke out. She glanced over the railing. Her family, the matchmakers and her friends smiled at them. Standing next to Ingrid, clutching a tub of popcorn, Lili waved.

The love in Noah's eyes took her breath.

He smiled. "Shall we make this the happiest happily-ever-after Truelove has ever seen?"

Chloe caught his face in her hands. "Let's."

And they did.

Chapter Sixteen

Three Years Later

Propped against the pillows, Chloe handed the baby to Noah. After the birth of their daughter earlier that morning, she was tired, but it was a good kind of tired.

Settling into the rocking chair beside the bed, he sang a soft, little song to the newborn in his arms.

"You don't mind that she isn't a boy?"

Looking up, he threw Chloe that crooked grin that never failed to make her knees wobble. "I adore girls."

The baby made a cooing noise.

"It's my privilege to be entrusted with the love and care of daughters." His blue eyes glinted with moisture. "And I never lose sight of how blessed I am to have their beautiful mother in my life."

On the table beside the bed, her phone buzzed. "Speaking of all your women in your life . . . Lili is on her way up with Mom and Dad."

Lili loved their home. She and Felix spent countless hours exploring the vast acreage of the property Noah bought just outside Truelove. Now a second-grader, she loved going to school each day and seeing her friends.

Chloe had continued her work with special needs children in her new studio at the Lyric. But her schedule and Noah's growing reputation as a preservation carpenter took a back seat to the needs of their family.

At last year's music festival on stage with Noah, Lili had performed her first solo on the violin. The father and daughter duo, especially the little girl with the child-sized instrument, had been a crowd favorite.

He also permanently endowed the Fliss Brenden music scholarship program at the Lyric Arts Center in honor of his late sister.

Noah eased out of the rocker and stood up. "Do you want to hold the baby?"

"I want my arms free to love on Lili first. She'll be missing us since we left for the hospital last night." Chloe smiled at him. "Just as I've been missing her."

"Thank you for loving her so well." He swallowed. "And for loving me."

She lifted her face for a kiss. "Loving Lili and loving you is truly the joy of my life."

Just as he kissed her, Lili, her pigtails flying, burst into the room. "Mommy? Daddy? Is my baby here yet?" A look of uncertainty crossed her delicate features. "Is it okay if I come see you now?"

"Hello, my darlin' girl." Chloe sat down on the bed and opened her arms. "I missed you so much."

Lili scrambled up beside her.

Noah held up the baby for Chloe's parents, who were close behind Lili. They exclaimed over the baby.

Lili snuggled against Chloe. "Pops bought me a cinnamon bun this morning from Madeline's."

"Wow." She chuckled. "How come you never bought cinnamon buns for the boys and me when we were little, Dad?"

He grinned. "'Cause grandchildren are extra special and meant to be spoiled."

"Lili," Noah beckoned. "Come meet your new sister."

Chloe squeezed her hand. "I know she can't wait to meet you."

Lili eased off the bed. Bending, he extended his arms so she could get a good look.

She did that little dance she sometimes did on her tiptoes, when she was feeling her happiest. "My baby's so bee-you-tiful. I love her."

Chloe exchanged a misty glance with Noah.

Lili held out her arms. "Can I hold her, Daddy?"

Noah gestured to the rocker. "Sit down first, please." Then he transferred the sleeping baby into Lili's arms. "Lili Felicity Brenden meet Isabella Ann Brenden."

Her smile went wide. "Hello, Bella Brenden." She planted a very sweet, very gentle kiss on the baby's forehead. "I'm your big sister."

Chloe's heart melted.

"I'm going to be the best big sister ever." Lili touched the tip of her finger to the baby's tiny nose. "Being the oldest is an important job. Uncle Jeff and I have so much to teach you."

Chloe cut her eyes at Noah. "God help us all," she sighed.

"He will." Noah's gaze lingered on hers. "Forever and always."

God was good. So very good. Because in Him, their hearts had found their truest home.

* * * * *

Dear Reader,

I always learn a lot from the stories God gives me to write. Chloe Randolph's always optimistic spin on life also inspired me to be more like her. Yet as she eventually realized, optimistic is not the same thing as faith-filled.

Here's what I'm learning about faith:

Faith means not getting what I longed for with my whole heart, and yet choosing to trust God anyway. Faith means hanging on to God—sometimes by the skin of my teeth—when His plans turn out to be different from mine.

God has been so faithful to me. I want to be faithful to Him. Even when I can't see His hand at work in a situation, I can trust His heart for me. He will always do what is best and right for me. I need not fear the future.

Thank you for sharing Chloe's and Noah's journey with me. It is through Christ we find our forever Home—the true happily-ever-after for which we were created. Thank you for telling your friends how much you enjoy the Truelove matchmaker series.

I'd love to connect with you. You can contact me at lisa@lisacarterauthor.com or visit lisacarterauthor.com, where you can also subscribe to my author newsletter for news about upcoming book releases and sales.

In His Love,
Lisa Carter